The Vengeance of the Mighty

The Dragon Warrior, Volume 3

Frank Spreader

Published by Frank Spreader, 2024.

This is a work of fiction. Similarities to real people, places, or events are entirely coincidental.

THE VENGEANCE OF THE MIGHTY

First edition. July 12, 2024.

Copyright © 2024 Frank Spreader.

ISBN: 979-8227403612

Written by Frank Spreader.

Table of Contents

To those who seek strength in adversity and find wisdom in
the unlikeliest of places.

For my family, whose love and support are my guiding light.

To the dreamers and warriors, may your battles be fierce, your
victories sweet, and your spirit unyielding.

And to the storytellers, who weave worlds from words and
inspire others to believe in the extraordinary...

Chapter 1

The Spirit's Lair

The gaping wound where his right hand had been steadily drained his strength.

Despite fleeing the Dimmitt graveyard with the desperation of a man pursued by hell itself, he now struggled to muster the energy for even a single step. His body lurched and swayed, as if manipulated by unseen forces, while his breath rasped in his throat—a desperate wheezing akin to a man nearing death's grasp.

He stood at the precipice, unsure how he had arrived there; the desolate landscape testified to its rare human visitors. A profound silence descended, sending a chill down his spine. His vision blurred, the world darkened around him, and his strength drained to its core. His body collapsed, plunging into the ravine as his foot snagged on a protruding rock at its edge. Fortunately, instead of a rocky abyss, dense undergrowth awaited below.

He tumbled downward, crashing through underbrush and catching on low-hanging branches. The pain was excruciating, heightened by the wound on his right arm stump. When he finally regained consciousness at the ravine's base, dusk had almost descended. The depths below were cloaked in darkness and cold, the last rays of sunlight failing to reach him where he lay.

He contemplated his situation, the throbbing agony in his swollen, bloodied right shoulder jolting his memory and bringing back the events that led him here. Hours earlier, he had engaged in a fierce battle with a formidable youth named Wintie Rayado. During that encounter, not only was he forced to flee, but he also lost his right arm, severed by his adversary. Amid the excruciating pain, a deep-seated thirst for vengeance simmered within him.

Living with only one hand, he was resolute in avenging the lifelong disability inflicted by Wintie Rayado. It wasn't until he gazed at the stars twinkling above that he realized night had fallen.

Kalin realized he couldn't stay sprawled there all night. He glanced to the right, seeing only bushes and wide-leaved trees in the darkness. Turning his head to the left, he initially saw nothing but darkness. However, amid the bushes, he faintly discerned a jutting rock at the ravine's base, roughly ten spear lengths away.

Kalin considered moving to the outcrop, but in his condition, the task seemed impossible. He couldn't muster the strength to crawl, let alone stand. Every inch of his body throbbed with agony, his limbs feeling as though they were coming apart at the joints.

With unwavering resolve to save himself, he gathered every last ounce of strength and inched closer and closer. Finally, Kalin reached the jutting rock, which turned out to be the mouth of a cave. As he reached the entrance, he collapsed into unconsciousness once again. When he awoke the following morning, several hours past sunrise, he was surprised to find his body feeling considerably better than the day before. Puzzled, Kalin wondered how this could be happening. As he attempted to move, he sensed that the strength he had exhausted the previous night was slowly returning. Sitting with his back against the cave wall, he felt a damp, tingling sensation creeping out of the cave. It seemed this air had influenced his state, gradually restoring his strength.

As he examined the cave walls around him, dimly veiled by thick, age-old dust, Kalin noticed countless inscriptions. The writings were haphazard and unordered, yet when pieced together, they formed a narrative that imparted a profound understanding of martial arts. Kalin's eyes widened as he took it all in. At first, what he read was difficult to grasp. These teachings were unlike anything he had ever encountered, detailing martial arts with peculiar and mysterious fundamentals, their lineage and style unknown.

As the sun climbed higher, Kalin felt his body improving, despite his hunched and staggering movements. Encouraged by the inscriptions on the outer walls of the cave, he ventured deeper inside. The air grew warmer and more humid, alleviating the tingling sensation in his skin.

Breathing in this air, Kalin felt rejuvenated, his chest easing. As he ventured deeper, he discovered more writings detailing unfamiliar swordsmanship teachings. Sadly, many of these instructional writings were either faded or too blurry to decipher. Nonetheless, the warm, tingling air felt increasingly comforting.

Kalin pressed on into the cave until his steps halted at an unbelievable sight. The cave culminated in a small pond, more akin to a pool, encircled by rocks. Its water was a deep blue, emitting a bluish vapor that possessed a magical, refreshing power over Kalin's body. In the center of the pool lay a smooth, blue stone, upon which rested a sword. The sword was severed, only two spans long, matching the depth of the water and the smoothness of the stone. This weapon, also emitting a blue light, was missing its pointed end. The mystery of why the sword remained severed and how it came to be there puzzled Kalin.

Standing at the pool's edge for a while, he felt his body grow increasingly refreshed. Inspecting the wound on his severed right shoulder, he noticed it was healing faster than before. *This pool water's got some mighty powerful properties,* Kalin pondered. He stooped to pick up the severed sword on the rock for a closer look.

However, halfway through his bend, his movement halted as his gaze fixed on the cave wall behind the pool.

Through the faint vapor, he could just make out a row of letters, somewhat difficult to read but still decipherable. The inscription read:

This cavern's known as the spirit's lair,
The pool's blue waters hold secrets rare,
The sword on the stone, a ghostly sight,
But now just a hilt and a tip so slight.

Who can find the missing blade's end,
And reunite it to transcend,
For he who masters this sword so grand,
Shall be the king of blades in the land.

Reading the inscriptions, Kalin surveyed his surroundings, from the cave's mouth to the pool's edge. The writings on the cave walls revealed a strange and ancient martial art and swordsmanship. Everything he found within the cave confirmed that it had once been the abode of a powerful being wielding the blue spirit sword. But why was the sword now reduced to mere remnants, and where was the rest of its blade?

Once more, Kalin stooped, his left hand within reach of the blue spirit sword. The moment his fingers closed around the hilt, a strange current flowed through him, restoring his strength and revitalizing his body. Not only that, but he felt lighter, and as he dipped his hand into the pool, he sensed a surge of new strengths and peculiarities.

Kalin was overjoyed. Without hesitation, he kneeled by the pool's edge and spoke aloud, "To the owner of this blue spirit cave, wherever you are, I'm Kalin, and I want to thank you. Your cave has healed me from the pain and wounds I've suffered today. I hope you'll consider taking me on as your student. I will diligently study everything written here."

Thus began his solitary pursuit, starting that day, delving into every inscription on the cave walls—martial arts and swordsmanship teachings that he endeavored to unravel alone, even the lost and unreadable parts.

Despite his efforts, Kalin could only grasp and comprehend a third of the knowledge about the spirit sword. Nevertheless, this achievement was already extraordinary.

Four months later, when he emerged from the spirit cave, Kalin had undergone a complete transformation in his martial arts knowledge. This bolstered his conviction that he would successfully pursue his vendetta against the Dragon Warrior, Wintie Rayado.

Chapter 2
Blade of Vengeance

Pursuing an enemy across the vast expanse of the New World was no easy task. They had to travel hundreds of miles, ascending and descending hills, crossing rivers, navigating jungles, and overcoming countless natural and man-made obstacles. In the brutal realm of the martial arts, finding the great foe could take months or even years and might never be achieved. The seeker might face perils along the way, potentially meeting their demise before exacting their vengeful wrath.

Kalin was aware of the challenges ahead but felt no fear about his newfound, albeit imperfect, knowledge. He was confident he could face everything on his quest to find Wintie Rayado, the Dragon Warrior, who had maimed his hands and left him crippled for life. Kalin had his own agenda for settling the score with the Dragon Warrior. He firmly believed in his ability to track down his formidable enemy and was equally convinced that his grand scheme for retribution would come to fruition upon encountering Lyvonte Bicette, also known as Supreme, in Nuevo Reino de León, the last known location of his former leader and martial arts mentor.

Upon arrival, Kalin was met with profound disappointment. The vengeance burning in his heart grew immeasurable when he discovered that Lyvonte Bicette had been killed by Wintie Rayado during a recent rebellion.

With his festering vendetta, Kalin departed Nuevo Reino de León, crossed Río Santa Catarina, and continued his journey to Cerro de la Silla. Near the mountain's base, atop Cerro de la Silla, stood the White Lotus School. Despite being only three years old, the school had already gained a renowned reputation extending to the Anahuac Valley. Its acclaim came not only from its founding principles of aiding the vulnerable and combating nefarious forces but also from its leadership by Willman, a martial arts master.

Over fifty years old, Willman had risen to fame in the martial arts realm over the past decade. Now, he perched atop Fisherman's Peak, engaged in deep meditation to deepen his spiritual understanding and cleanse himself of past transgressions. He passed the leadership of the school to his oldest, most adept, and most trusted student, Gabrielito Kuilan. At that moment, the White Lotus School exuded an air of tranquility. Inside the spacious house, the eight students—six males and two females—sat in solemn silence, cross-legged, listening intently to Gabrielito as he read from a book authored by their teacher. The book explored the literature of spiritual, mystical, and worldly life. Gabrielito's voice was clear and soothing, ensuring that every piece of advice and lesson he imparted was readily grasped by his seven fellow disciples.

"In the course of life," Gabrielito Kuilan read aloud, "every individual will inevitably pass through three stages: first, the moment of their birth into the world; second, the span of their life on this earth; and third, the moment they depart this world, returning to their origin or meeting their demise."

As Gabrielito Kuilan continued reading, laughter and jovial chatter could be heard outside the large house, accompanied by lively conversation.

"Born into this world, live our days, and eventually kick the bucket, ha ha ha."

The booming, disdainful voice reverberated with such force that it startled all the students of the White Lotus School, including Gabrielito Kuilan. All heads turned toward the door, where a grimy, unkempt man with a menacing demeanor and a missing right arm stood on the threshold.

"Who are you, brother?" Gabrielito Kuilan asked, briefly examining the unfamiliar guest. He remained seated, unruffled, with the book still resting on his lap.

"No need for questions yet," the man at the door cut in, grinning nastily. "I ain't finished talking."

Some of the White Lotus School students looked intrigued, shifting in their seats, but Gabrielito Kuilan subtly signaled them to wait. The man at the door kept speaking, pointing with his left index finger at the book in Gabrielito Kuilan's lap.

"What's written there, what you read earlier, is all true—birth, life, death. But do y'all know that everything written and read earlier is what you'll experience yourselves today?"

"What do you mean, brother?" Gabrielito Kuilan asked calmly, unruffled.

The man with the missing arm laughed loudly. "It's all useless to have that book. It's pointless to own it if you don't grasp the meaning of my words. You've been born and lived your lives in this world, but you've never experienced death or tasted dying. Well, today, to prove the truth of that silly book, I, Kalin, am willing to help you understand what it's like to die."

Gabrielito Kuilan stood up from his seat, closed the book on his lap, and handed it to one of his fellow disciples. "Brother," he said calmly, "in this world, there are many with twisted minds. I fear you may be one of them, lost and finding yourself here."

Kalin's laughter ceased abruptly. His expression hardened, and his jaw muscles tightened. His left hand drifted to his waist, and in an instant, it wielded a blade—a stump emitting a blue glow, a mystical blue sword at first glance. Though blunt, the students of the White Lotus School recognized the potency of the sword in the hands of the unknown man who called himself Kalin, understanding its danger even without a tip.

Suddenly, Kalin let out a loud scream and sprang forward. The stump of his sword stirred, emitting a blue light as it slashed sideways.

Without hesitation, Gabrielito Kuilan countered with a strike of his empty hand, infused with high internal energy. To his surprise, the blunt sword in his opponent's hand caused the wind of his internal energy strike to deflect to the side.

"Brothers!" exclaimed a student of the White Lotus School. "A lost man like this doesn't need to be faced one-on-one. Let's take him down together."

"Everyone, hold your ground," shouted Gabrielito Kuilan. "We must uphold the honor of our school and honor the legacy of our teacher. Let us remain true to the chivalrous spirit of the martial world."

Gabrielito Kuilan's words were cut short as Kalin launched another attack, employing a peculiar maneuver.

Despite Gabrielito Kuilan's skill, he managed to evade most of the attack, but the blunt end of Kalin's blue sword grazed his chest, slashing his clothes. In that moment of contact, Gabrielito Kuilan felt a surge of heat through his body.

Kalin chuckled darkly. "This stump of a sword, this blue ghostly blade, carries a lethal poison. In three hours, your life will be forfeited."

Gabrielito Kuilan and his fellow disciples were taken aback. He unsheathed a dagger from his waist, followed by his companions doing the same. Without a word, the eight students of the White Lotus School, each armed with a dagger, closed in on Kalin, who wielded the mystical blunt sword.

Kalin chuckled wickedly. "You'd be better off ending yourselves than meeting your demise with the blade of my mystical sword."

"The mystical sword," murmured the students of the White Lotus School to themselves.

They had heard of the sword's prowess from their teacher, though rumors said it had vanished years ago, only to reappear in its current blunt state, its power seemingly undiminished. Regardless of the weapon their opponent wielded, Willman's students felt no fear or hesitation. All eight charged forward, their daggers gleaming as they aimed for Kalin's vulnerable spots.

Kalin grimaced and let out a loud bellow. His body flickered, surrounded by a surge of blue light from his sword. Three screams echoed almost simultaneously, and three of Gabrielito Kuilan's fellow disciples collapsed; their lives abruptly ended.

Gabrielito Kuilan gritted his teeth in frustration. His blood boiled with anger, but the wound had drained his strength, leaving him devoid of his inner energy.

Gabrielito Kuilan fought with all his might, but his opponent's swordplay was formidable, its moves difficult and unpredictable. With each strike, two more of his fellow disciples collapsed lifelessly.

Seeing this, Gabrielito Kuilan shouted to his two female disciples, "Wuendy, Nuvia, quickly leave this place! Run fast, save yourselves!"

But both girls, despite their delicate appearance, had hearts of true grit.

Wuendy responded, "Our lives and deaths are bound together with you, Brother Gabrielito."

The girl darted swiftly and delivered a quick thrust to her opponent's neck.

Kalin laughed, tilting his body to avoid the dagger thrust. In that moment, his left leg moved, and Gabrielito Kuilan's final male disciple was flung against the wall. His chest caved in from Kalin's kick, his heart and lungs burst, and his life fled.

Gabrielito Kuilan was by then depleted of energy. The wound on his chest and the poison from the mystical sword had taken a profound toll, coursing through his veins.

He knew he would soon follow his fallen disciples. Once again, he shouted a reminder: "Wuendy, Nuvia, run before it's too late!"

"These pretty girls aren't going to get far; the tip of my mystical sword has already sealed your fate." Kalin chuckled wickedly. "But before you die, I'll give you both a taste of the world first."

Gabrielito Kuilan, understanding the meaning behind his opponent's words, shouted a warning once again. However, the two girls paid no heed and attacked fiercely.

Kalin dodged nimbly several times and then, with remarkable speed, struck Wuendy and Nuvia with the pommel of his weapon. Both girls fell motionless.

Aware of the impending disaster about to befall his fellow disciples, Gabrielito Kuilan summoned his remaining strength and all his might, lunging at Kalin from the side.

Spinning around, the one being attacked retorted, "Your death is right before your eyes; your demise is right in front of your nose—it's better to commit suicide."

"Accept my dagger first, wicked man. We bear you no enmity; why such excessive cruelty?"

"Enough already; I'll silence you now," Kalin said.

The mystical blue sword slashed at Gabrielito Kuilan's abdomen. Willman's disciple leaped, evading the blade, but in mid-leap, the opponent's weapon surged faster, now aimed at Gabrielito Kuilan's face, leaving him no escape.

In a desperate bid for survival, Gabrielito Kuilan pressed the dagger against his own face. The maimed blue phantom sword continued its onslaught. Both grappled fiercely, seeking advantage. Fireworks erupted as Gabrielito Kuilan's blade shattered under the relentless assault. Staggering back, blood flooded his face, his knees buckling and his waist twisting in terror.

Gabrielito Kuilan slumped to the floor, then sprawled, exhaling his last breath with all his might. Gripping the broken dagger, he hurled it toward Kalin, but this feeble attack was easily dodged.

Kalin chuckled, wiping the bloodstains from the broken blue phantom sword before tucking it back behind his waist. He pivoted, his eyes sparkling as he surveyed Wuendy and Nuvia, both standing stiff and powerless after the earlier paralyzing attack.

"Hehehe, no need to rush to meet your end," Kalin said, extending the tip of his tongue to wet his lips as he advanced toward Wuendy.

His left hand moved, ripping the school uniform worn by the girl. Her chest lay wide open, white, smooth, and solid. Kalin's body was engulfed by a roaring desire. His left hand moved, moved, and moved again.

Chapter 3

The Unveiling of Dragon Fire Axe Warrior

Meanwhile, atop Fisherman's Peak, on the nineteenth day of his unwavering meditation, Willman's mental focus faltered abruptly. His attempts to quiet his mind and shut out external distractions began to unravel. Despite his determined efforts, the more he concentrated, the more resistance he encountered. Eventually, the martial arts master, seasoned with half a century of practice, reluctantly opened his eyes after nineteen days of deep meditation. His contemplative gaze scanned the familiar landscape—the wilderness, hills, river, sun, sky, and clouds—all unchanged since his arrival. Yet, an unsettling unease gripped his heart, driven by an instinctual feeling that something significant had transpired beyond his mountainous perch, despite the serene, unaltered vista before him.

He rubbed his face wearily with both hands before slowly descending from the weathered black rock where he had sat in deep meditation. The worn surface of the rock bore testament to both Willman's enduring inner resolve and the passage of time.

He wiped his face again, pondering, *Perhaps something's happening at the school.* Willman mused quietly.

With the swift execution of the running technique, the old man's form vanished from the cave's entrance in an instant.

He reappeared racing down Fisherman's Peak, swift as the wind, his astonishment at the doorstep of the grand house so profound that Willman stood frozen for a moment. Eventually, his trembling form thawed from its petrified state.

"Who in the Lord's name is responsible for this?" he muttered. "What grave sin have we committed to deserve such a calamity?"

His disciples lay scattered in every direction, lifeless and drenched in blood. Yet, what pierced the heart of the White Lotus School's leader were his two female disciples, Wuendy and Nuvia. They sprawled on the floor of the grand house, exposed, with daggers piercing their throats and blood covering them from neck to chest and down to their thighs.

Willman closed his eyes, unable to bear the sight any longer. Despite his efforts to steel his heart, tears still escaped from beneath his closed lids. His throat tightened, suppressing the urge to sob.

For years, he had mentored his eight disciples, fought alongside them to uphold truth, and battled against immorality and wickedness. Yet now, facing their horrifying deaths, Willman struggled to believe the extent of the tragedy with his eyes shut tight. The leader of the White Lotus School attempted to ponder and speculate on who could be responsible for such a vicious calamity against his disciples.

He couldn't fathom it, couldn't comprehend it, and for as long as he could recall, he had never made an enemy in the martial arts world. Willman's eyes fluttered open once more.

In that instant, through his tear-blurred vision, he fixated on a large notebook of his own writings, skewered by one of his disciple's daggers. The book's cover bore a series of sentences written in blood.

·

To the head of the White Lotus School,

·

If you aim to avenge the deaths of your disciples, come to the peak of Mount Shasta on the 13th day of the 12th month.

.

Dragon Fire Axe Warrior,
Wintie Rayado.

.

Willman's eyes, brimming with tears, narrowed, causing the previously suspended tears to trickle down and moisten his cheeks. His thoughts drifted back decades to a time when the martial arts world was dominated by a supremely powerful figure, unmatched in prowess. That figure was Sinforosa Chiflada, a female warrior wielding the mystical Dragon Fire Axe. Her name held sway among the white-clothed martial artists, revered as the Dragon Warrior, a vanquisher of evil and champion of the weak.

For the black-clothed faction, however, she was undoubtedly a formidable presence. During the Dragon Warrior's lifetime, before Willman founded the White Lotus School, there had been no enmity or conflict between them—they had both fought for the same cause. Thus, the bloody events unfolding today, culminating in the challenge letter signed by the name Dragon Fire Axe Warrior, left Willman perplexed.

What is the significance and connection of the name Wintie Rayado? The leader of the White Lotus School pondered deeply, his thoughts turning to the events of decades past, when the martial arts world trembled under the might of the Dragon Warrior.

Abruptly and mysteriously, Dragon Warrior vanished, sparking wild speculation among martial artists. Some believed she had intentionally withdrawn from the martial arts world, while others feared she had met an untimely end. Amid lingering uncertainty, the tragic events at the White Lotus School now convinced Willman that something significant had indeed befallen Sinforosa Chiflada, the renowned Dragon Warrior.

He deduced that Dragon Warrior had been defeated in a great, unknown battle by a newcomer named Wintie Rayado. It seemed plausible that Dragon Warrior had met her end at the hands of Wintie Rayado, who then claimed the Dragon Fire Axe and adopted the mantle of Dragon Fire Axe Warrior. The leader of the White Lotus School's thoughts then turned to the mystery of Wintie Rayado's identity. The name was unfamiliar, yet Willman was certain that neither he nor the White Lotus School had ever harbored animosity or vendettas. The motives behind the mass murder of his disciples remained deeply obscure to Willman, but as he gazed at the blood-written challenge, a fire ignited within him. The twelfth month was still nine months away. Would he wait that long to confront and settle the score with Wintie Rayado, or would he leave the school immediately to track down his formidable foe?

However, Willman knew that his immediate task was to bury the bodies of his eight disciples in the schoolyard.

Chapter 4
The Pact with Taon Luttrell

Between Río Sacramento to the north and Río San Joaquín to the south lay a land of remarkable fertility, akin to nature's own cornucopia. The fields rolled in lush waves, yielding crops of such abundance that they bordered on the supernatural. Granaries overflowed, ensuring the villagers could thrive for years without want. Their existence surpassed that of neighboring communities, characterized by robust health and industriousness. At the heart of this region stood the village of Sacramento, renowned for its unparalleled prosperity. Here, fields and fish ponds teemed with bounty beyond measure. Leading them was Chief Kuiper, a wise and capable leader whose governance was so revered that chiefs from distant villages sought his counsel on matters of community and prosperity.

On a chilly evening, Chief Kuiper, still spry at forty-five, sat on the steps of his modest home. Beside him, his wife, Wanzella Sinnott, engaged him in conversation, the dying embers of his tobacco pipe casting a soft glow.

"It's quite chilly tonight, dear," remarked Wanzella Sinnott, adjusting her clothing to shield her fair calves from the cold.

"Looks like rain. Let's go indoors," Chief Kuiper suggested, rising to his feet.

But before the couple could reach the door, three swift black shadows darted past. They were of average height and muscular, with grim and menacing visages.

Seeing this, Chief Kuiper, sensing danger, quickly reached for the dagger at his right hip. Yet, with startling speed, one of the figures in black swung a machete at his neck. As Wanzella Sinnott tried to scream, another assailant silenced her with a hand over her mouth.

Chief Kuiper realized that these three individuals were unmistakably part of a nefarious gang of robbers. It was the first time such malefactors had dared to set foot in their village during his stewardship, which had always ensured the safety and tranquility of their community.

Despite his shock, Chief Kuiper steadied himself and asked, "Who are you, and why have you come here?"

The assailant, who had swung the machete at Chief Kuiper's neck, grinned chillingly, his teeth gleaming as darkly as his attire.

"Ah, that's a good question. But before I answer, remember this: if you misbehave or disobey us in any way, don't be surprised to find your son, who is sleeping inside, impaled on the house post."

Chief Kuiper was startled.

Wanzella Sinnott trembled as the man in black grinned once more.

"Now, as for who we are, have you heard of the infamous Black Trio gang from Río Colorado?"

Chief Kuiper's face paled.

"Right now, you're facing them, Kuiper. I'm Taon Luttrell, their leader," he declared.

Chief Kuiper was well aware of the notorious Black Trio gang from Río Colorado, infamous for their vicious and malevolent robberies along the river, extending to the border. Río Colorado lay far from the village of Sacramento, and Kuiper couldn't fathom how these depraved individuals had ventured so close.

"Taon Luttrell, if robbery is your intent, make it quick. Take what you want and leave swiftly."

The leader of the Black Trio chuckled.

"We've gained notoriety as robbers, but today, Chief Kuiper, our purpose here is not theft," Taon Luttrell declared.

Naturally, Chief Kuiper found this statement perplexing. "Then what brings you here?" he asked.

"We've come to negotiate with you," he said.

"What kind of agreement?"

"From now on, you must obey our every command, understand?"

Chief Kuiper's throat tightened.

"What are you implying?" he asked.

Meanwhile, his right hand stealthily returned to his waist.

Chief Kuiper, determined to resist despite Taon Luttrell's machete at his neck and his wife held captive, swiftly gripped his dagger and thrust it into Luttrell's stomach.

Yet Luttrell proved more cautious than expected. With a quick motion, weapons clashed, sparks flew, and Wanzella Sinnott's muffled cry came from behind her gag. Luttrell's machete clashed against Chief Kuiper's dagger, severing the tip of his thumb up to the nail.

Chief Kuiper groaned in pain as blood streamed from his severed thumb, Taon Luttrell's machete still pressed against his neck.

"I suppose you're asking to have your neck cut off real quick, huh?" Taon Luttrell snapped.

"Go ahead; I'm not afraid of you, you bunch of thugs," Chief Kuiper retorted defiantly.

The leader of the Black Trio delivered a sharp slap to Kuiper's cheek with his left hand, causing his vision to swim. Kuiper's cheeks flushed red, and the corners of his lips split and bled.

"You still feel like running your mouth?" Taon Luttrell asked, his tone mocking.

Chief Kuiper growled inwardly but kept his silence.

"Will you listen and follow my orders, or will you choose death?"

"I'm not afraid to die, and neither is my wife," Chief Kuiper replied firmly.

Taon Luttrell grinned. "You might not fear death, but can you bear to watch your son inside have his head roll on this floor?"

Chief Kuiper lapsed into silence.

Taon Luttrell pushed Chief Kuiper inside and gestured for him to take a seat. "For your life and your family's, let's have a civil conversation, Chief. Starting today, you'll obey me. I want to know when you collect taxes from your people every month."

Chief Kuiper didn't fully grasp the intent behind the question, but he responded, "First Monday of every month."

"After you collect those taxes, where do you hand them over?" Taon Luttrell asked again.

"To the mayor in Sonoma, who then forwards it to the capital city," Chief Kuiper replied.

"Well, that's a good rule, but next month's tax collection will be ten times the usual amount," Taon Luttrell stated firmly.

Chief Kuiper was taken aback, and his surprise deepened as Taon Luttrell elaborated on his earlier statement.

"You'll collect that tax three times a month, understand?"

"What kind of rule is that?" Chief Kuiper was bewildered.

"Don't worry about what kind of rule it is; just do as I say," Taon Luttrell replied dismissively.

"You can't simply do as you please, Taon Luttrell. If you overstep, you'll answer to the mayor of Sonoma and perhaps even the kingdom," Chief Kuiper asserted sternly.

"Handling the mayor and the kingdom is your concern. But if you dare to report this to anyone, I'll come after your entire family, understand?" Taon Luttrell threatened.

"You may target my family, Taon Luttrell, but you won't get away with challenging the mayor and the kingdom," Chief Kuiper retorted defiantly.

"I've already told you that handling the mayor and the kingdom is your issue. What matters to me is that three times a month, I'm expected to collect a sum that's ten times what you've been taking from the village," Taon Luttrell stated firmly.

"This is outrageous, Taon Luttrell! None of the villagers can afford to pay such a steep tax," Chief Kuiper exclaimed in disbelief.

"People around here are quite prosperous; they have fields, cattle, cows, goats, chickens, and even ducks," Taon Luttrell remarked.

"But ten times more—"

Taon Luttrell interjected sharply, "Do I need to push you to collect fifteen or twenty times more?"

"I won't carry out your orders, Taon Luttrell. I can't burden the villagers like that," Chief Kuiper asserted firmly.

"I don't care if you can't squeeze the villagers. Are you willing to watch your son die?" Taon Luttrell challenged coldly.

The leader of the Black Trio's menacing threat forced Chief Kuiper into silence.

Taon Luttrell nodded to one of his men by the door, who, upon receiving the signal, promptly entered Chief Kuiper's bedroom.

Kuiper stood abruptly. "What are you planning to do?" he snapped.

Taon Luttrell pushed Kuiper back into his seat forcefully. Moments later, his henchman returned to the room, now carrying Kuiper's four-year-old son, who slept soundly, unaware of the situation. Wanzella Sinnott and Kuiper exchanged worried glances.

"What are you planning to do with my boy?" Kuiper asked urgently.

"As long as you do as I say, your boy will be safe and sound. I'm taking him for now as insurance that you won't go running your mouth to anyone. Understand, Chief Kuiper?" Taon Luttrell explained firmly.

Chief Kuiper remained silent.

"You understand?" Taon Luttrell repeated, his voice sharp.

Chief Kuiper reluctantly nodded, a gesture of reluctant acquiescence.

"You'd better hand over those taxes no later than a day after you collect them. Take them to an old shack at the crossroads to Sonoma. I'll be waiting there myself at noon sharp," Taon Luttrell instructed sternly.

"I won't deliver them," Chief Kuiper said firmly. "You can come here yourself."

Taon Luttrell chuckled coldly. "Don't forget about your boy's safety, Chief," he warned.

The leader of the Black Trio from Río Colorado then gestured and, with his two henchmen, promptly exited Chief Kuiper's house.

Chapter 5

The Tyrant's Burden

Last night, Wanzella Sinnott wept incessantly, tears flowing in an unending torrent of sorrow. Her eyes were inflamed, resembling swollen red orbs, burdened with unseen grief.

Chief Kuiper paced restlessly, unable to sleep, his steps devoid of purpose. His heart churned with anxiety over his son's abduction by Taon Luttrell and his gang. Under the surface, a fierce, unrelenting anger simmered, overriding any concern for his own or his wife's safety.

He remembered, with a pang, that their son was their only child. The tax issue gnawed at Chief Kuiper's mind, threatening to push him toward madness.

He dared not bring this matter to the mayor of Sonoma or the governor if he wanted to ensure his child's safety. The only option seemed to be obeying Taon Luttrell's unreasonable demands, but what about the villagers' reaction? The tax burden was already heavy, and they would surely accuse him of profiteering, risking unrest. If he had to levy taxes ten times the usual amount for Taon Luttrell, plus the regular dues for Sonoma's mayor, it would mean an unbearable elevenfold increase.

If not for a desperate plea to the Almighty, he might have considered ending it all with his dagger, but he knew that wasn't the answer. This morning, he reluctantly had his assistant announce to the villagers that next month's tax collection would increase elevenfold. This was supposedly aligned with the governor's strategic vision for progress and maintaining a strong military, though it was a flimsy pretext crafted by Chief Kuiper to mask the harsh reality. As word spread, discontent surged through Sacramento's populace. Voices rose in condemnation, labeling it as blatant oppression and extortion, justified only in the name of progress and military might. Must the people be burdened by such excessive taxes? they asked, eyeing their growing obligations warily. Some village elders sought out Chief Kuiper, but he avoided them, bewildering those who once saw him as benevolent and wise. Inside his home, the constant weeping of Wanzella Sinnott, his wife, filled the air—a mystery to the elders. As the first tax collection day arrived, a significant number of people refused to pay. Wrestling with turmoil, the chief threatened dissenters with apprehension and capital punishment. Reluctantly, the populace complied in the second collection, though not without chaos quelled by Chief Kuiper. Yet, as the third collection neared, rumors of rebellion spread, threatening to erupt into violence.

Unable to place blame on the townsfolk, one night Chief Kuiper slipped away to Sonoma to meet Mayor Bodie Servello in secret. There, he recounted the unfolding events in full detail.

Bodie Servello appeared visibly startled as Chief Kuiper bid him farewell. Assuring him with a promise to dispatch a contingent of soldiers posthaste, Bodie Servello pledged his support. However, as the third tax collection approached, not a single soldier materialized.

Chief Kuiper found himself bewildered and at a loss. As signs of rebellion grew more pronounced, he stumbled upon Taon Luttrell on the outskirts of the village in his fleeting bewilderment.

"What brings you to me, Chief?" asked Taon Luttrell, gnawing on barbecue just cooked up by his boys.

At that moment, the Black Trio from Río Colorado found themselves at the edge of the forest.

"You're saying there's a problem?" Taon Luttrell asked. "You know tomorrow's the day we collect that tax money, and you better hand it over at the crossroads to Sonoma."

"I believe myself to be in trouble, and this situation of mine is connected to your extortion," replied Chief Kuiper.

Taon Luttrell chuckled, tossing the bone from his meal near Chief Kuiper's feet. "Regarding this trouble, have you paid a visit to Mayor Bodie Servello in Sonoma?" Taon Luttrell asked, rising from his seat on a fallen log with a chuckle.

Chief Kuiper was taken aback, his expression shifting. He wondered if this bandit chief knew about his journey to Sonoma to meet Mayor Bodie Servello. Taon Luttrell's laughter escalated, filling the air. His face took on a more sinister aspect, catching Chief Kuiper off guard. Suddenly, the bandit leader slapped him across the cheek.

"Taon Luttrell, you scoundrel!"

Taon Luttrell's slap struck Kuiper's face for the second time.

"Quit yappin'," he barked. "Shut your trap."

"But, Taon Luttrell—"

"I told you not to go blabbin' to anyone, and you ran to Mayor Bodie Servello. You forgettin' the price your boy's gonna pay."

Chief Kuiper's face turned pale.

"What did you do to my boy, Taon Luttrell?"

"Now you're all shook up, aren't you, you damn fool? Mayor Bodie Servello sent five of his men to Sacramento, but I caught them halfway. All five met their maker because of your stupidity."

"My boy, how's he doing?" Chief Kuiper asked, his voice a blend of tears and pleading.

"I'm being kind enough to forgive your mess-up this time, but don't expect forgiveness in the future."

Chief Kuiper's chest heaved.

Upon reflection, he might have noticed the peculiarity in Taon Luttrell's words today compared to three weeks ago.

Back then, Taon Luttrell had threatened to kill his son if Chief Kuiper reported to the mayor or governor, which he had done with Mayor Bodie Servello. Oddly, Taon Luttrell was now offering forgiveness. However, by doing so, the gravity of his crime had not only reached the mayor's ears but would undoubtedly be forwarded to the capital city, especially following the murder of the five soldiers.

"Now, tell me about this trouble you're talking about, Chief," said Taon Luttrell.

"The villagers will revolt tomorrow if I continue collecting that outrageous tax," said Chief Kuiper.

"You used to say you weren't afraid of dying, but now your life is in danger. Why are you suddenly seeking me out?"

Chief Kuiper gritted his teeth.

"Head back to Sacramento, Chief. We're coming there tomorrow," said Taon Luttrell.

"I hope there won't be any violence."

"That's our business; there's no need for you to get involved," said Taon Luttrell.

"Can I see my boy, Taon Luttrell?" Chief Kuiper asked.

"Not this time, not yet," the bandit leader replied calmly.

The chief of the Sacramento village fell into a contemplative silence.

Moments later, he walked unsteadily to his horse and climbed onto its back. Before riding off, Chief Kuiper asked, "Taon Luttrell, how long will you continue this tyranny?"

Taon Luttrell chuckled. "Don't ask too many questions. You better start thinking about your fate tomorrow. The villagers might have already turned against you by the time we arrive."

Chapter 6

Dawn of Reckoning in Sacramento

From the secluded corners of the village, the distant crows of roosters echoed, their calls reverberating through the stillness of night. The chill of midnight had dissipated, yielding to the crisp dawn signaled by the brightening eastern sky, marking the end of night and the arrival of morning.

Chief Kuiper, the village elder, struck a match and brought it to his pipe, igniting the tobacco with a soft hiss. His face was gaunt, his eyes sunken, and his complexion pallid, yet within the shadows of his visage smoldered an ember of fierce resentment, fueled by the tobacco's bitter bite on his tongue.

For years, he had spat on the ground, but lately, the bitterness on his tongue had intensified. His meals were increasingly sparse, and with each passing day, restlessness and anxiety consumed him. Chief Kuiper's greatest fear was that the townsfolk would arrive before the Black Trio from Río Colorado.

He kept glancing out into the yard, unsettled by the morning's silence. Replacing the pipe between his lips, he drew in a deep breath before exhaling a cloud of smoke. Again, he spat on the ground and wiped his lips. Startled by approaching footsteps, he twisted to find his wife behind him. Her once robust frame had diminished, mirroring his own gauntness, and her complexion was pallid.

Wanzella Sinnott, once renowned for her striking beauty, now obscured by clouds of worry, agonized over her child's safety and the imminent arrival of the townsfolk. Her husband's fate weighed heavily on her mind as she awaited the arrival of the chief of Sacramento's assistant, who was due to collect taxes that day.

However, he was notably absent on this occasion. How could he summon the courage to appear, knowing well that today the villagers were poised for revolt?

"I really hope those folks don't show up around here."

Chief Kuiper chewed his lip, knowing his wife's words echoed his own wishes. Yet he was painfully aware that these hopes were futile. The townsfolk were coming. They would arrive.

He knew. He was certain.

Wanzella Sinnott glanced out into the yard again before stating, "If they do come, I suppose we can't continue hiding the evil deeds of those three cursed individuals. We must confess to the townsfolk before they turn against us."

"My life's worth no more than a dime, Wanzella," Chief Kuiper murmured. "I'd sacrifice it all, but it means nothing if we can't secure our child's safety."

The solitude persisted for a while.

Suddenly, Wanzella Sinnott grasped her neck tightly and exclaimed, "They're coming, they're coming!"

Chief Kuiper lifted his head and peered into the yard, confirming his wife's words. A group of men from the village emerged around the bend in the road, obscured by tall reeds. This assembly consisted solely of village leaders, numbering no less than a hundred.

Though their weapons were not visible from a distance, Chief Kuiper knew some must be carrying concealed arms. Soon, the spacious yard was filled with villagers, the air buzzing with their voices. Chief Kuiper and his wife stood motionless on the porch, their eyes scanning the people of Sacramento. Finally, a villager stepped forward, ascending the steps to stand a few paces from Kuiper.

Kuiper was familiar with this man.

He was Kraigg, a farmer from the eastern village. As he ascended the steps, silence fell over the place like a shroud.

"Chief," Kraigg said, breaking the silence. "You know why we're here."

Kuiper stayed silent, noticing a sardonic smile on Kraigg's face.

"Understand that I stand here today as a representative of many in Sacramento," Kraigg gestured behind him, continuing, "those who, for the past month, have suffered extortion, oppression, and burdensome taxes nearly eleven times what they should be."

"Kraigg," Chief Kuiper interjected, "get to the point. What do you want?" Again, Kuiper noticed a mocking smile curling Kraigg's lips.

"What we want, we've already told you since you first imposed that outrageous tax."

"I'm not personally in favor of this, but it's an order from above, a directive from the governor for the development and upkeep of the troops."

"Orders from above are just that—orders. If your boss told you to jump into Río Sacramento, would you do it? Every directive needs to be logical, Chief."

Kuiper's face turned red, while Wanzella Sinnott began to sob uncontrollably.

"Kraigg, perhaps this tax collection is only temporary."

"Yeah, temporary, alright, but it'll only end when every last one of us in Sacramento is dead from these damn taxes."

"I understand that tax is a significant burden."

"If it's such a burden, why enforce it?" Kraigg shot back.

Chief Kuiper bit his lip again, torn between revealing the true motives behind the tax collection and explaining who was truly responsible for the exorbitant demands. Yet the thought of his only child in the hands of the Black Trio from Río Colorado held him back.

"We folks from Sacramento demand the repeal of these insane tax rules," Kraigg stated.

"I don't have the authority to do that, Kraigg."

"You can convey that to the mayor in Sonoma, and he can relay it to the capital. If you're unwilling to do so, we won't hesitate to take matters into our own hands," Kraigg said.

"Are you attempting to intimidate us?"

"You could say that, Chief."

"Brother Kraigg," Wanzella Sinnott's voice rang out, "you don't understand, you just don't."

"We know more than you think," Kraigg snapped. "What we've uncovered is beyond our worst expectations. Chief Kuiper, your husband, is nothing but a two-faced tax collector, seeking glory above all else and draining the life out of the people below. We know more than you do."

"I suggest you show some respect, Kraigg." Chief Kuiper interjected, stung by the accusations of flattery and extortion.

Kraigg turned toward the crowd and chuckled.

Meanwhile, a villager shouted, "Why waste time talking with that snake in the grass? Shut him up with a machete!"

Kraigg turned back to Kuiper. "Did you hear that shout, Chief?" he asked.

Kuiper's lips moved silently.

"If you want that tax repealed, go speak to the governor in the capital yourselves."

"Then what's the point of you being the chief around here?" yelled another villager.

"Is it all just for show?" yelled another villager.

"Just for show and squeezing us dry!" yelled another.

Then another villager shouted, "We don't believe this tax is from the governor. It wouldn't surprise us if it's just some crazy rule you made up yourself."

More shouts followed, causing Kuiper's face to flush and his ears to ring.

"Kraigg, I hope you'll take your people and leave," said Kuiper.

"Yeah," Kraigg sneered, "we'll leave once you declare that the insane tax rules are over from now on."

"No one has the authority to overturn a decision made by the governor," Kuiper replied.

His voice was loud, but his words lacked conviction.

"Well then, it looks like we'll have to use force," Kraigg said.

"Are you defying the government, Kraigg?" Chief Kuiper asked, hoping the question might help him escape the dire situation.

But Kraigg's only response was a derisive smirk.

"Don't try to intimidate us with government talk, Chief. We all know that taxes are yours, not the government's. The government has always been fair and wise," Kraigg said, stepping up to Chief Kuiper with clenched fists.

Several Sacramento residents also stepped onto the platform.

Chief Kuiper took a few steps back.

Wanzella Sinnott screamed.

"Kraigg, what are you up to?"

"We're trying to seek justice the right way, but you're pushing for violence," Kraigg replied.

His right hand moved suddenly, triggering a cacophony of horse whinnies and chaotic scattering among the people in the front yard.

"In the name of the government, if you are not looking to die, you all better scatter!"

Several screams echoed as people were kicked by their horses.

Three riders leaped from their mounts with effortless grace, swiftly positioning themselves between Kraigg and Chief Kuiper. Clad in imposing soldierly attire, their expressions grim and formidable, the trio appeared. Chief Kuiper, Kraigg, and the Sacramento townsfolk were equally taken aback.

Chief Kuiper, amid his shock, felt a measure of relief in recognizing the three as Taon Luttrell and his two cronies. Yet, what puzzled the Sacramento chief was why these brigands were dressed in military attire.

As Taon Luttrell faced Kraigg with hands on hips, he declared, "We Sonoma soldiers reckon you're the cause of all this commotion."

Kraigg and the Sacramento locals were stunned, while Chief Kuiper and his wife simmered silently, observing the Black Trio's adept performance as impostor soldiers, manipulating the townspeople, and hiding their nefarious extortionist history.

Kraigg suppressed his surprise. He felt no fear of the trio posing as soldiers; was this not the perfect moment to expose Kuiper's tax extortion? "Friends," Kraigg said, "if you are indeed soldiers, that's quite the coincidence."

"What do you mean by coincidence?" Taon Luttrell snapped.

Kraigg proceeded to explain the tax issue to Taon Luttrell in vivid detail, but he was astonished by Taon Luttrell's response.

"So, you're leading the people of Sacramento down your own path of violence; that's rebellion, that's defying the government, and that's going against the governor's rules. This tax matter comes directly from the governor, relayed through the mayor in Sonoma."

"Why is it that only the folks in Sacramento are being taxed like this?" questioned a resident standing next to Kraigg.

"Yeah, other towns aren't!" shouted another voice from outside the yard.

"Do you all understand what this is?" Taon Luttrell snapped. "This is the governor's decision. Sacramento isn't like those other villages. That's why it's only fair they bear a heavier tax burden."

"Quite a burden," jeered a resident.

Kraigg then intervened to calm the tense atmosphere. "We're not opposing the governor or rebelling in any way. We simply want the tax to be reverted to its previous level," he said.

Taon Luttrell spat on the floor. "You're the smooth-talking troublemaker, whispering sweet nothings to your townsfolk. You can talk tough to the chief, but don't try to lead the entire town. Leave. Get out quickly," he said.

So Kraigg responded, "We came here from Sacramento to seek justice. If we must leave, then justice must have already been served."

"Oh, is that how it is?" Taon Luttrell grinned.

His large, dark brown teeth appeared repulsive.

"Before you start preaching about justice, try taking my right hand first," Taon Luttrell said, slamming his hand into Kraigg's chest.

The one struck quickly leaped aside, but Taon Luttrell's left hand found Kraigg's stomach; the earlier strike with his right hand had been a feint.

Kraigg twisted and staggered backward, clutching his aching stomach. A wave of nausea washed over him, threatening to make him vomit as he struggled to catch his breath in short, tight gasps. It was evident that this man was more than just a farmer; he possessed skill in martial arts.

With controlled breathing and focused energy, he swiftly launched into an attack. Six other residents joined him, and chaos ensued. Four residents were knocked to the ground, two lost consciousness, and two suffered broken collarbones and dislocated elbows.

Meanwhile, as Kraigg was thrown against the stair railing, Taon Luttrell struck him in the chest.

He struggled to rise, trying to steady himself for a counterattack, but before he could act, his vision blurred, and he vomited thick, clotted blood. Moments later, his body collapsed on the floor, sparking chaos among the bystanders. They rushed up the stairs in disarray, armed with various weapons.

"Anyone who wants to meet their maker, come on up!" yelled Taon Luttrell, swinging his machete.

The attackers hesitated in their assault, but those who pressed on recklessly met a grim fate. They lay scattered and bloodied, struck down by Taon Luttrell and his cronies. Despite their overwhelming numbers, the remaining onlookers hesitated to intervene further.

Wanzella Sinnott fled into the house, screaming in terror, while Kuiper bit his lip and closed his eyes, unable to bear the horrific scene.

If it weren't for his son's safety, he would have drawn his dagger and joined the fight long ago.

"Anybody else want to meet my machete? Step right up," said Taon Luttrell, pushing his hand toward his hip and chuckling. "If you don't have the nerve to face the mess on these stairs, it's time to leave."

The anger of the residents surged, but what unfolded before them caused their courage to falter and sent chills down their spines.

Chief Kuiper stood motionless, his jaw clenched tight with anger. His hatred for the Black Trio from Río Colorado was immeasurable, yet like the people of Sacramento, he felt powerless to act. The residents tended to Kraigg and the other casualties.

Before they departed, Taon Luttrell called out, "I don't want to see this kind of mess again, unless you're asking for it like your friends did. Anyone feeling rebellious is welcome; my machete's been thirsty for blood for a long time."

Taon Luttrell's statement was met with silence.

Disguised as a soldier, Taon Luttrell shouted, "Remember, by noon tomorrow, make sure that tax is paid. Anyone who tries to argue knows the consequences." Once the Sacramento residents had dispersed, Taon Luttrell sheathed his machete and addressed Chief Kuiper: "You owe me for saving you from a noose, Chief."

Chief Kuiper muttered quietly under his breath, his jaw muscles tense and bulging.

Taon Luttrell laughed heartily. "By sundown tomorrow, make sure that tax money is delivered to the old cabin at the crossroads on the way to Sonoma."

Kuiper remained silent.

"Hey, are you going deaf on me?" Taon Luttrell asked.

Yet the chief of Sacramento remained silent.

So Taon Luttrell barked, "Are you going deaf or something?"

"I'm not deaf, Taon Luttrell."

"Why aren't you saying anything, huh? Maybe you're mute," taunted Taon Luttrell.

Two of Taon Luttrell's henchmen grinned smugly.

"By sundown tomorrow, I better have that money, you hear?" Taon Luttrell demanded.

"What if the folks refuse to pay?"

"I don't want to hear excuses about paying or not paying. Tomorrow, I just want the money," Taon Luttrell signaled to his two henchmen.

The trio descended the stairs of the house and walked toward their horses.

Chapter 7
Confrontation at Moonlit Bridge

That night, Kraigg summoned all his strength and limited medical knowledge to mend his internal injuries inflicted by Taon Luttrell's blow. It wasn't Kraigg's martial prowess that facilitated his recovery, but rather the fortunate circumstance that Taon Luttrell's morning strike hadn't been as severe as it could have been. Amid his animosity toward Taon Luttrell and his allies, his intense hatred for Chief Kuiper, and the looming tax payment, these pressures converged upon him.

That night, despite his recent recovery, Kraigg resolved to journey to the capital. He confided his plan to a few companions, and together with four others on horseback, they set off for the capital city. The night was pitch dark, with only faint starlight and a crescent moon struggling to pierce the gloom.

Kraigg and his four companions rounded a bend and approached a bridge crossing the river. At that moment, they spotted a group of horsemen on the opposite side. Three riders halted their horses, eyeing them with unease.

Kraigg halted his horse in the middle of the bridge and signaled to his four companions to stop. Despite the pitch-black night, Kraigg's eyes could discern the figure of the foremost horseman ahead. To his dismay, it was one of the soldiers who had confronted him earlier that day.

"Damn," muttered Kraigg. "How did these rascals find out about my journey to the capital city?"

Until then, neither he nor his companions had any idea who the three figures blocking the end of the bridge were.

The horseman in front, none other than Taon Luttrell, chuckled. "Seems like the lesson and warning I gave y'all earlier today didn't quite stick, huh?" snapped Taon Luttrell.

Kraigg remained silent, his right hand slipping behind his back to grip the hilt of his machete. His four companions mirrored his cautious stance. Across the bridge, Taon Luttrell's laughter echoed briefly, followed by a shout that pierced the night.

"Where do you think you're going, huh?"

"We have no quarrel with you. Step aside and let us pass," said Kraigg calmly.

"Ask for a path, and you can pass through," said Taon Luttrell, nudging his horse aside.

The invitation left Kraigg and his companions motionless atop their horses, stunned into silence.

"Come on, why aren't y'all moving?" asked Taon Luttrell.

Kraigg hesitated, uncertain.

"If that's how it's going to be, then it'll be your sorry souls crossing this bridge," Taon Luttrell declared, unsheathing his machete with two distinct metallic sounds as his companions followed suit.

Seeing this, Kraigg and his comrades quickly drew their own machetes.

"I know you're heading to the capital," Taon Luttrell said, tugging on his horse's reins. "But just so you know, it's only your sorry souls that will meet the governor at the palace."

In the span of two spear throws, Taon Luttrell's horse surged forward with a powerful kick, followed by his two henchmen. Three machetes flickered in the dim moonlight. Five more awaited them. Sparks flew as the blades clashed, cries of pain echoing. Two of Kraigg's companions fell from their mounts—one with a gut wound, the other losing his right arm to a swift strike from the Black Trio of Río Colorado, still disguised as soldiers, launching another relentless assault. Two more screams rang out as they collapsed, one toppling into the river. Thrown from his horse, Kraigg's machete slipped from his grasp, yet he emerged unharmed.

Realizing further engagement was futile, he swiftly turned and made his escape.

Taon Luttrell laughed heartily. "You sly one, where do you think you're sneaking off to?"

From his belt, the leader of the Black Trio from Río Colorado drew a dagger. It sailed through the air with a sharp whistle.

Unaware of the looming danger, Kraigg pressed on with his flight. Just inches from his back, the venomous dagger nearly struck true. Suddenly, from the shadowy undergrowth by the river's edge, a star-shaped object gleamed silver-white and shot forth. The burst of fireworks not only startled Taon Luttrell, causing his poisoned dagger to miss its mark, but also shattered the dagger in two.

Startled, Taon Luttrell momentarily abandoned his intent to kill Kraigg and spun around, his sharp eyes fixed on the direction from which the silver-white star-shaped object had come.

The leader of the Black Trio from Río Colorado shouted, "You meddling devil's spawn, come out and face my daggers!" With those words, Taon Luttrell hurled three poisoned daggers simultaneously into the darkness of the bushes.

A whistling sound echoed, followed by mocking laughter.

"I'm right here, mate. Why attack the empty air?" remarked the man mockingly.

"Cursed bastard," Taon Luttrell spat, hurling another pair of daggers with his left hand toward the man standing about six spear lengths away on the riverbank.

The figure at the river's edge met the oncoming attack with a single, fluid motion of his left hand. In that instant, both poisoned daggers ricocheted harmlessly away. Taon Luttrell's shock was palpable; a stifled cry escaped his lips as he witnessed the eerie precision of the man's movements.

"Who do you think you are, picking a fight like that?" he snapped, discreetly signaling to his two boys to prepare to surround the intruder.

The man inquired, "What's all this commotion about here?"

"Hey, you long-haired fool," cursed one of Taon Luttrell's henchmen. "You dare talk back to Sonoma soldiers?"

"Well, aren't you the Sonoma soldiers?" scoffed the man at the river's edge. "Last I heard, Sonoma boys aren't fond of violence, let alone killing folks who look like this."

Meanwhile, Kraigg, on the verge of making his escape, sensed a new commotion behind him. He turned his head slowly, then pivoted his entire body, coming to a halt behind a tree. What he saw next was nothing short of astonishing.

"We don't need to hide from this human-faced monkey," Taon Luttrell declared.

"Well, it's better to be upfront," retorted the man by the river. "Just come clean about who you all are."

"Before you learn who we are, you'd better drop to your knees and beg for forgiveness," Taon Luttrell said arrogantly.

"Hey, why's that?"

Thinking Kraigg had already escaped and was nowhere to be found, Taon Luttrell stated, "Just so you know, the Black Trio from Río Colorado doesn't let troublemakers who meddle in our affairs live."

"Oh, so you're the Black Trio from Río Colorado, those fierce, inhuman bandits. No wonder your faces are black as coal," he jeered.

"Damn it, you've got my machete!" yelled Taon Luttrell's henchman on the right. With a swift motion, he leaped from the horse's back, his machete flashing toward the young man's head.

The young man stood firm, strangely composed, even laughing.

Then, in a sudden burst of speed, he leaped backward. Taon Luttrell's henchman's attack missed, causing him to stumble and lose balance. Before he could recover, a kick landed squarely on his rear end.

"People who don't know how to mind their own business deserve what's coming to them." Seeing his comrade and henchman being humiliated to the point of kneeling, Taon Luttrell and his remaining henchman leaped from their horses. "Tell me your name first, you fool," Taon Luttrell barked, "or your spirit's going to leave for no good reason."

"Your talk is too big. If you want to know my name, step up."

With a sneering laugh, Taon Luttrell surged forward. His machete lashed out swiftly while his left hand, like a sledgehammer, struck toward his opponent's solar plexus. This was the berserk wind style, the rage of a fallen tree, truly formidable.

"Well, it looks like you've got some tricks up your sleeve too, huh?" mocked his opponent. He dove to evade the machete swipe, then leaped sideways to dodge the oncoming fist.

Moving with remarkable speed, his open right hand slipped between the two attacks, thrusting toward Taon Luttrell's forehead. The head of the Black Trio from Río Colorado was no fool; otherwise, he would have been useless as the feared leader of the gang for years along the Río Colorado and the border.

With a fierce shout, Taon Luttrell made an extraordinary move. His body sprang upward like a spear, and in that leap, his right leg surged toward his opponent's face. Simultaneously, from behind, his henchman's machete aimed for the young man's back. The target of the attack whistled sharply.

"Ah, it looks like you're really after me, but I reckon it's not my time yet."

The young man darted forward, his knees buckling and his hands twisting like serpents. Taon Luttrell's henchman toppled backward, vomiting blood and sprawling on the ground.

Taon Luttrell groaned in pain as his opponent's arm struck his shin bone. Meanwhile, the henchman, who had been kicked in the rear, got back up and launched a ferocious attack. However, luck wasn't on his side either; his opponent darted forward, and his machete met a hard elbow. The second henchman crumpled to the ground, clutching his injured leg.

Seeing both his men laid out like this, Taon Luttrell felt as though he were in a nightmare. Had his gang finally met their match?

For years, he had roamed and led the Black Trio from Río Colorado, but never before had he seen his men taken down in a single clash. Even he felt the sting of the young stranger's hand—a youth he didn't recognize at all. Seething with rage, Taon Luttrell channeled his inner strength through his right arm into his machete, his left hand gripping three poisoned daggers. His stance widened, his waist bent slightly forward, the hand clutching the daggers raised up and back, while the machete in his right hand extended straight ahead.

"Ever seen this move before, you damn punk?"

"Ah, just a move like scattering flowers to stab the fruit; even the oldest lady could recognize it," the young man retorted.

Taon Luttrell was not only angered by the taunt but also surprised that his opponent could anticipate his next move. To hide his surprise, Taon Luttrell said, "You know the name of this move well, but understand that this is your death sentence. It's best to tell me your name now so you don't die wondering."

"Quit yapping and show me the greatness of that move you're relying on."

Taon Luttrell chuckled icily. His body hunched even lower, almost imperceptibly, as he swiftly launched the three daggers held in his left hand toward the young man. The first aimed for the base of the neck, the second nicked his chest, and the last thudded into his lower abdomen. The speed and accuracy of the daggers, thrown with his non-dominant hand, were both impressive and lethal.

As the poisoned daggers flew toward his face, Taon Luttrell surged forward, swinging his machete. The wind from the machete's swing added to the daggers' speed, a move known as *scattering flowers to pierce the fruit*. The attacks came in quick succession.

"Your move ain't half bad," said the young man, "but try blocking my palm first."

The young man slammed his left hand into Taon Luttrell's face, a fierce wind striking and propelling the three daggers.

Taon Luttrell cried out in alarm as two of the daggers, redirected by the wind and the opponent's strike, turned back toward him. Unable to evade them, Taon Luttrell was forced to use his machete to knock them aside. The two poisoned daggers shattered and were flung far.

In the midst of deflecting the daggers, Taon Luttrell momentarily neglected his defense. As he adjusted his stance, the young man's right palm dangerously approached his head. The head of the Black Trio from Río Colorado attempted to chop at the opponent's arm with his machete, but was too slow. The young man's left arm swiftly slipped in, striking the joint of his elbow.

Taon Luttrell groaned and staggered backward, his arm broken from the strike. The blow to his forehead from the opponent's palm was searingly painful, leaving his skin bearing the likeness of a dragon's fiery imprint.

Taon Luttrell tried to gather his inner energy and regulate his blood flow, but his strength seemed to wane. Cold sweat drenched his body, his forehead throbbed with pain, and his vision blurred. His knees trembled beneath him.

"Damn," muttered Taon Luttrell under his breath.

"You've still got a mouth on you."

"If I fall for your trap today, don't think you've beaten me, young man. One day, I'll hunt you down and snap your neck," Taon Luttrell declared, grabbing three daggers and hurling them with his left hand. Swiftly, he flung the weapons at the young man and spun around to make his escape with equal speed.

The young man leaped to the side. Two daggers sailed past him, one to his left and the other to his right, while he deftly swatted away the third with a wave of his left hand.

Then, with a tap of two fingers from his right hand, he sent a signal and called out, "Why the rush? I wasn't finished talking to you earlier."

Immediately, Taon Luttrell's body stiffened, making him immobilized and unable to move. The young man chuckled and turned toward the large tree by the riverbank.

"Hey, buddy hiding behind the tree, come on out. I want to have a chat with you too."

Kraigg, hidden behind the tree, was startled. However, knowing the young man wasn't part of an evil group, he stepped out without hesitation. Taon Luttrell's earlier confession that he and his companions were the infamous Black Trio from Río Colorado gave Kraigg even more reason to delve deeper into the situation.

"Hey there, what happened here earlier with you and your friends?"

"It's a long story, but first, if you don't mind, what's your name?"

"I'm Wintie," the young man replied.

"I'm Kraigg. My friends and I, also from Sacramento Village, were heading to the capital city," Kraigg explained. He recounted everything, from the burdensome taxes imposed by Chief Kuiper to the tragic deaths of his companions.

Wintie, also known as Wintie Rayado or Dragon Warrior, shook his head. "I've heard of that notorious gang led by Taon Luttrell. It's no surprise they've been hiding out around here. They're known for causing trouble along Río Colorado."

"And I suspect these crooks are either working together or are Chief Kuiper's henchmen."

"Could be," replied Dragon Warrior. "But they might also be the ones extorting the village head."

Kraigg nodded in agreement.

"Let's clarify things by questioning this guy," said Wintie Rayado. He moved closer to Taon Luttrell, ready to confront the leader of the Black Trio, but before he could act, a figure suddenly emerged from the darkness.

The figure seized Taon Luttrell by the waist and swiftly whisked him away into the darkness.

Kraigg was stunned.

Dragon Fire Axe Warrior shouted, "You sneaky thief, stop!"

In response, raucous laughter echoed from the person carrying Taon Luttrell. "Wintie Rayado, you foolish youth, don't think you're the only skilled one in this world. I'll be waiting for you tomorrow afternoon in the Sonoma Marsh. I hope you have the courage to accept this invitation to your demise. Ha ha ha!"

"Hey now, hold up. Who are you?"

"Tomorrow afternoon, Wintie."

With fury, Dragon Warrior unleashed a punch toward the unfamiliar man. A tremendous and unforeseen gust of wind assailed the stranger. In that instant, a streak of blue light halted Wintie Rayado's punch as if striking a steel wall, leaving Dragon Warrior stunned. The strike, delivered with nearly a third of his inner strength, was deflected by the stranger. This reinforced Wintie Rayado's suspicion that the man who had abducted Taon Luttrell might be his teacher, a fellow student, or perhaps even a sorcerer from the dark arts allied with Taon Luttrell.

Chapter 8

Reckoning at Sacramento

The Sacramento village head's yard glowed brilliantly in the night, illuminated by numerous torches. The townsfolk, unable to contain their impatience any longer, were eagerly prepared to administer justice. Standing bound to the hitching post were Taon Luttrell's men, subdued by the Dragon Warrior's prowess. They had been awoken by the post and ensnared as well by Wintie Rayado's enchantment.

Kraigg stood beside Chief Kuiper, a few spear lengths away from Wintie Rayado's composed figure. He had just briefed the village elders on all he knew about the pair and the recent events near the river's edge by the bridge. Chief Kuiper's gaze shifted between Wintie Rayado and Taon Luttrell's henchmen. In that moment, the Sacramento village head struggled to contain his emotions, momentarily forgetting about his son in Taon Luttrell's grasp and the fugitive Taon himself still at large.

"My fellow Sacramentans," Kuiper declared, stepping boldly into the crowded assembly, "it's time to lay bare the truth behind this taxing ordeal. With a heavy heart and countless grievances, I've had to bear the accusations you've thrown my way. You call me an extortionist, and I accept it. You label me a leech, a tyrant, and more; I'll own up to it all. But tonight, you need to hear the real story from me—the truth behind this burdensome tax. I once claimed it was mandated by the governor for military needs. Now, I confess, it was all a facade—a grand deception I orchestrated to shield my family and spare you from the unseen violence and injustices."

The residents of Sacramento exchanged puzzled glances, their faces mirroring shared confusion.

Chief Kuiper wiped his face and continued, "You all heard Kraigg's account earlier, which vindicates me. But let me provide further context. Those two bound men are henchmen of the Black Trio gang from Río Colorado, led by the notorious Taon Luttrell, who escaped with assistance from an unknown accomplice. They are not soldiers, as they falsely claimed this morning. One night, they came to my home and coerced me into collecting taxes ten times higher than usual. This meant I had to collect taxes eleven times in total—ten of which I had to surrender to them, while the usual one was forwarded to Sonoma, and from there, to the capital. I resisted, but given their leverage over me—especially since they held my only child captive—I had no choice but to comply, lest they harm him. You can see now that I cannot deny this truth any longer, unless you wish for my son to face dire consequences."

The night was as silent as a graveyard. The residents stood in stunned silence, completely caught off guard, until their collective anger erupted in a resounding roar.

When a voice in the crowd shouted, "Cut down these two bastards," the people of Sacramento surged forward, brandishing their weapons.

Yet in that moment, the Dragon Warrior advanced, his voice resonating with deliberate authority, aiming to sway the enraged crowd. "Hold on, everyone. These scoundrels will face justice, but consider the chief's son. Allow me a moment with one of them."

Had Kraigg not enlightened the townsfolk about the true identity of the long-haired youth, they might have dismissed Wintie Rayado's words, given the young man's silent yet profound sway over them.

Wintie approached the henchman bound on the right-hand side. "What's your name, buddy?" he asked.

The man remained silent, his eyes shifting with a gaze filled not just with hatred but with a personal vendetta that seemed to pierce through the tense atmosphere.

"Oh, it looks like my handiwork rendered you speechless, huh?"

"Enough with the chatter. The day of reckoning from my leader, Taon Luttrell, will come. All of you here will be sent to hell."

A grin spread across Wintie Rayado's lips.

"Maybe you and your buddy will be the first to be chopped up into mush by the folks," Wintie Rayado interjected. "No need to boast about your leader; he's already skipped town with a companion."

This revelation startled Taon Luttrell's two henchmen. Since waking up, they hadn't seen their leader and had no idea where he was.

And Wintie added, "I suspect you're connected to the mayor over in Sonoma. Just come clean."

Taon Luttrell's henchmen remained silent.

"Say it," Wintie demanded sharply.

Instead, the man defiantly spat on the ground.

"Shut him up!" Kraigg shouted, unable to contain himself.

"You're not going to talk?" the Dragon Warrior inquired.

Once more, Taon Luttrell's henchman spat defiantly on the floor.

Wintie chuckled as he approached a torch held by one of the residents. "Ever felt the warmth of a fire?" he asked, amused. "Your tough demeanor would look even more impressive in the glow." With that, Wintie Rayado teasingly brought the torch closer to the man's face.

Taon Luttrell's henchman remained immobilized, paralyzed with pain. Agonizing cries filled the air relentlessly. The night breeze now carried the acrid scent of singed eyelashes, eyebrows, and patches of his hair. His facial skin blistered and reddened from the flames.

"Want another round?" Wintie asked, chuckling.

"I swear, if I break free, I'll hunt you and your kin for seven generations," Taon Luttrell's henchman snarled, seething with anger.

"Don't be ridiculous. You're not getting out of here. And even if you do, it might just be your spirit, because I don't have any descendants yet," the young warrior chuckled.

Whether they wanted to or not, many people witnessed it and ended up chuckling along.

"Tell me. What's your connection with the mayor of Sonoma?" Wintie demanded, holding the torch closer to the man's face.

"Nothing there," Taon Luttrell's henchman replied tersely.

"Ah, this is just a lie or a fib," he scoffed dismissively.

"I'm not lying, not at all," he insisted.

"So what was the point of pretending to be soldiers this morning?"

"That's none of your concern," he replied.

"Oh, I see. While it might not be my concern, it certainly concerns this torch," Wintie replied.

And once more, the torch flame kissed the man's face.

He screamed in agony.

Wintie waited patiently for a few seconds. "Are you going to talk, or do I need to keep asking?" he pressed.

"I'll explain," the man finally conceded.

A smile crept across Wintie's face.

He withdrew the torch slightly. "Now, speak up so everyone can hear you loud and clear."

So, Taon Luttrell's henchman began to speak: "Mayor Bodie Servello from Sonoma sent a messenger to us. He proposed an extortion scheme. He offered us a deal to collect the tax, agreeing to split the proceeds fifty-fifty. Our leader accepted the offer and—"

"Understood," Wintie Rayado said simply.

Chief Kuiper stepped forward and stated, "So Mayor Bodie Servello orchestrated this entire scheme."

"Indeed."

"Let's catch that mayor!" the crowd shouted.

"Just hang him with these two scoundrels!" others yelled.

The Dragon Warrior raised his left hand. "I'll handle the mayor," he declared. "Right now, our priority is rescuing the chief's son."

Chief Kuiper's blood boiled at the thought of his son; he grabbed hold of Taon Luttrell's henchman by the hair.

"Where is my boy?" he demanded.

The man laughed cruelly, his blistered and reddened face showing no remorse. "Don't count on your son surviving, Kuiper," he taunted.

Kuiper snapped, gripping the man's head. "Where is he?"

"Maybe he's already dead, thanks to my leader," the man sneered.

Kuiper's hand shot out, seizing the torch from Wintie Rayado. A scream ripped from Taon Luttrell's henchman as the torch surged toward his right eye. It ruptured, with blood seeping down his blistered, charred face.

"I'll blind your other eye too, you scoundrel, unless you tell me right now where you're keeping my son," Kuiper threatened.

The man knew that once caught in such a manner, survival was unlikely. It seemed pointless to resist providing information. Yet, in the desperate mind of Taon Luttrell's henchman, a glimmer of hope for escape always lingered. The menacing threat of blinding both his eyes forced his hand, and he revealed the information. The child was being held captive in an ancient temple in Vacaville, bringing some relief to Kuiper.

"But," he warned, "if I arrive and my boy isn't there or I find him dead, don't expect to see another sunrise."

"Now, whatever happens to these two scoundrels isn't my concern anymore. Just do your best not to harm him until the chief's son is found safe. As for Mayor Bodie Servello in Sonoma, leave him to me. Tomorrow, you can retrieve his body from Sonoma, but I can't promise he'll still be breathing. That will depend on his choices. If he survives, it's up to you to escort him to the capital. Farewell."

"Wait a moment," Kraigg called out, almost simultaneously with Kuiper.

However, the Dragon Fire Axe Warrior had already dashed through the crowd of Sacramento residents and melted into the night's darkness. In the ensuing calm, the eerie silence shattered as the shadowy figure of the Dragon Warrior dissolved into obscurity. With his disappearance, the residents of Sacramento swiftly forgot his warning and descended upon Taon Luttrell's hapless henchmen, bound and defenseless. Their fate was sealed by the darkness that enveloped them. Countless weapons and a torrent of steel rained down on the pair, yet not a sound escaped their lips—no cries, no moans. They faced their grim reckoning for their sins, exhaling their final breaths as their bodies lay soaked in blood, their faces so mangled they were unrecognizable.

Chief Kuiper didn't wait to see what the people of Sacramento would do next. With Kraigg and three others, he rode out of town, heading for Vacaville—an isolated, rarely-visited lookout about thirty miles away. The only building in Vacaville was an ancient temple, as described by Taon Luttrell's men. Despite the darkness, finding it wasn't difficult.

Chief Kuiper ignited the torch he carried and, accompanied by the four others, ventured into the ancient temple. Discovering his child in a dire condition, Kuiper felt a surge of relief and joy—his only child was still alive. The boy lay asleep on grimy tiles, dressed in clothes stained with filth. His form was emaciated, his skin pallid from neglect, and his hands and feet were bound.

Kuiper kneeled and embraced his child.

Kraigg loosened the bonds around the child's wrists and ankles, and the youngster immediately became alert. Tears of joy streamed down Chief Kuiper's cheeks.

Chapter 9
Taon Luttrell's Debt

Elsewhere, Taon Luttrell felt his rigid body being carried into the night by an unknown figure. Faint moonlight filtered through the trees along their path, casting a dim glow.

He was puzzled and contemplative, unsure of the identity or intentions of the stranger bearing him away. Yet, recalling the man's demeanor and his actions and words toward the long-haired youth earlier, Taon Luttrell reassured himself that this man meant no harm, quietly easing his mind. Then he asked, "Hey buddy, who are you?"

"There aren't many answers for you right now," replied the man carrying him.

His voice was rough and gravelly.

He moved with the swiftness of the wind.

"Where are we heading?" Taon Luttrell asked again.

"I told you, don't ask anything if you ain't getting it," he replied.

Consumed by curiosity, Taon Luttrell complied, keeping silent for the duration of their journey. The singular detail he gleaned about his mysterious bearer was the man's truncated right arm, severed at the shoulder. Their path led them to a small pond, where the one-armed man came to a halt.

Taon Luttrell was lowered and leaned against a tree by the pond's edge. The man then removed the restraints from Taon Luttrell's body.

"Get your breath right and find your inner strength," said the one-armed man.

Taon Luttrell acted swiftly, proceeding with his intent, guided by the teachings of martial arts from any tradition. Using his one hand, the man deftly treated Taon Luttrell's broken arm and bandaged it with a strip of cloth.

"I owe you my thanks and my life," said Taon Luttrell gratefully.

The man who helped him chuckled softly.

"There's a debt and a credit," he said, chuckling softly. "A favor given; a return expected."

"What are you getting at, bro?" asked Taon Luttrell.

"One day, I'll come to collect on the help I gave you."

Taon Luttrell frowned. "You don't have to call it in, but if the opportunity arises, I'll definitely repay you. And once I'm healed, if you're game to join me in Río Colorado, I'll set you up with cash, jewelry, or whatever else you desire."

The man with the amputated arm grinned, revealing teeth stained a dark brown.

"I don't need all that," he muttered. He briefly touched the bandage on Taon Luttrell's arm, and suddenly, Taon Luttrell felt a powerful surge of inner strength coursing through his body.

His body felt invigorated, and the pain in his broken arm subsided.

"Thanks," said Taon Luttrell. "Mind sharing your name? I'm Taon Luttrell."

"I know who you are. I've heard about your crew causing a stir along Río Colorado, and when I found out you were in these parts, I had a mind to meet you."

"What exactly are you getting at?" asked Taon Luttrell.

"Like I mentioned earlier, there's a debt and a credit, a favor and a return. Someday, I might need your assistance."

"Don't worry, I'll be there. But what do you need me for?"

"You don't need to know why just yet, but you'll find out. Listen up: on the thirteenth day of the twelfth month, you need to be at Mount Shasta."

"Mount Shasta, huh?" Taon Luttrell echoed.

"Yep, about eight months from now. And remember one thing: don't try going back to Sacramento to square things with Chief Kuiper. You might run into the bastard who messed you up earlier. For now, you can't face him. There'll be a time to settle scores with him, so you need to come to Mount Shasta on the thirteenth day of the twelfth month. Got it?"

Taon Luttrell nodded in understanding. "Any idea who this bastard might be?" he asked.

"You've figured it out," the man replied.

Taon Luttrell was startled as he touched his forehead. There was no pain, but the skin felt slightly rougher than before.

"Take a look at the pond."

Taon Luttrell crawled over to the edge of the pond. Leaning in close to the clear water, under the faint light of the stars and crescent moon, he noticed a dragon faintly etched on his forehead. Taon Luttrell gazed in awe at the one-armed man, then turned to scrutinize his reflection in the pond. He rubbed his forehead, trying several times, but the dragon wouldn't fade. Wetting his forehead with pond water, he rubbed it repeatedly, yet the dragon persisted.

"No matter what you try or how you attempt it, that dragon won't vanish from your forehead, Taon Luttrell. It's etched there with a palm infused with inner strength and great power. You could peel the skin down to the bone, and that dragon would remain, ingrained in your skull."

"Who's that young man with the long hair who knows about the dragon?" Taon Luttrell inquired once more.

"His name's Wintie Rayado, and he's quite a powerful guy," replied the one-armed man. "But," he added, "when the thirteenth day of the twelfth month arrives, his time will be up."

Silently, though the one-armed man didn't elaborate further, Taon Luttrell now understood that there was a web of vengeance entangling the one-armed man and the young man with long hair who had injured him.

"Over the next eight months," the one-armed man added, "you should focus on honing your martial arts skills even further."

Taon Luttrell nodded in agreement.

The one-armed man said firmly, "Now we part ways. Remember the thirteenth day of the twelfth month, and don't even consider disobeying my orders."

"Where are you heading, buddy?"

"I've got plenty of business to take care of."

"But you haven't told me your name yet."

"My name's Kalin."

Chapter 10

The Intruder's Game: Sonoma's Night of Surprises

Sonoma greeted him with an eerie silence as he arrived, the day slipping into late evening's embrace. The frigid air, sharp as knives, pierced to the bone.

At a dimly lit tavern, he paused to quench his thirst and thaw his bones with a steaming mug of spiced wine. Amid the gritty ambiance, he sought Mayor Bodie Servello's residence, an easy find. It stood prominently as Sonoma's grandest edifice, emanating a serene aura. Two sentries stood watch at the entrance, while inside the foyer, several men lingered, indicating the mayor's current guests.

Ignoring the guards flanking him, he strode forward confidently. "This is Mayor Bodie Servello's place?" he asked one of the sentries.

"What can I do for you?" the guard responded.

"Ah, it's nothing, just curious," the young man replied, ruffling his long hair. "Is the mayor in?"

"He's occupied with guests. Who are you, and what do you need?"

"Just curious," the young man replied, scratching his hair again before resuming his stride without another word.

"Damn," muttered the guard.

The damned individual kept walking.

"Crazy guy," one guard said.

Both guards watched until the young man disappeared around the dark street corner.

Thirty minutes later, when the young man returned, the guests at the residence had disappeared. The grand lamp in the foyer had been replaced with a smaller one.

Seeing the young man approaching again, one of the guards snapped, "Hey, what are you doing back here?"

"Get out of here before I knock you with the butt of this spear," the other one growled.

The young man grinned.

"Listen, everyone," he said.

Both hands were raised to his face, and the index and middle fingers were extended.

"You all see these fingers?" he asked.

"You nutcase, keep moving or I'll bash your head in!" the guard yelled, his spear pointed threateningly.

"Ah, don't get your britches in a twist. I ain't finished talkin' yet," the young man replied, unfazed by the guard's threat.

His fingers stayed extended.

"See if you all can count these fingers I'm holding up," he said.

Naturally, the two guards became increasingly exasperated by the young man's antics and words. In a swift motion, the butts of their spears swung toward his head. However, before the spears could connect, the young man's hands shot out, striking the nerves at the base of their necks. Instantly, they fell silent and stiffened, paralyzed. The young man chuckled triumphantly.

He hoisted both guards onto his shoulders and walked into the courtyard of the residence. Tossing them into the horse stable behind the house, he then entered through the unlocked back door. Inside, a middle-aged woman, busy washing dishes as a household maid, was startled to see the unfamiliar young man with long hair.

He grinned at her warmly.

"Who are you?" she inquired, eyeing him cautiously.

The young man's smile remained.

He waved his left hand, and a sharp breeze grazed the woman's neck.

She was about to scream, but her voice was swiftly silenced as her body froze, immobilized by a precise nerve strike. The young man calmly led her to an empty room at the rear of the building.

At that moment, Mayor Bodie Servello emerged from the restroom, only to be taken aback by the unexpected sight. To his astonishment, a muscular, long-haired young man he didn't recognize was sitting comfortably in his rocking chair, eyes closed as if in blissful repose.

What in the world? How did someone get into my building? Mayor Bodie Servello thought to himself.

The young man in the chair continued to rock back and forth, his eyes still closed.

"Who are you?" The mayor thundered, his voice echoing off the walls of the room.

The rocking chair swayed gently, mirroring the relaxed posture of the young man seated in it, eyes closed in serene repose.

Mayor Bodie Servello seethed with fury. With determined steps, he advanced toward the rocking chair and its occupant. His right palm was poised to strike; he swung with force, but just as his hand was about to connect with the young man's cheek, the young man's eyes snapped open.

In an instant, he leaped up as if propelled by a spring, effortlessly floating two spear-lengths away from his seat. Mayor Bodie Servello's hand missed its mark and struck the back of the rocking chair instead, shattering the backrest into countless splinters that scattered across the room. The sheer force behind the blow left one wondering about the consequences had it landed on the young man's cheek.

"Well, well, if it isn't Bodie Servello," the young man said, rubbing his eyes. "I was just catching some shut-eye, and here you come, bothering me."

"What are you doing here? Do you want me to chop your head off?" Mayor Bodie Servello snapped, his fury palpable.

During his tenure as mayor, today marked the first time someone had addressed him simply as Bodie Servello. The young man chuckled lightly and, seemingly unfazed, settled back into the rocking chair. It resumed its gentle sway as he closed his eyes once more.

"Blasted luck," Bodie Servello grumbled.

With a swift movement of his right foot, the rocking chair collapsed into a heap of splintered wood. In the blink of an eye, the young man leaped and stood in a corner of the room near a small table.

"You've got quite the talent for wrecking chairs, don't you, Bodie Servello?" the young man asked, grinning.

Meanwhile, the commotion in the living room drew out Bodie Servello's wife, who emerged not only surprised but also shocked by what she saw.

"What's going on, dear? Who is this person?" the woman asked.

"Babe, get the guards!" Bodie Servello shouted at his wife.

The woman yelled, urgently summoning the guards, but none appeared. Unbeknownst to her, the two guards had already been incapacitated by the young man in the horse stable.

Bodie Servello seethed with fury as he watched the long-haired young man casually take his cigar, light it from the box on the small table in the corner, and start puffing away. His jaw clenched tightly.

He squeezed and released each of his right-hand fingers, one by one. Soon after, they turned red, the color spreading up to his elbow.

"You stray mutt, your luck's run out today. You're going to meet your end with a blow from my iron fist," Bodie Servello declared.

The red hand descended upon the young man's face. A sudden gust of warm wind rushed forward unexpectedly. The young man's body flickered and shimmered. Bodie Servello's wife screamed. The wall where the young man had been standing was shattered, pockmarked, and charred. Meanwhile, the person who had been attacked was now calmly puffing on a cigar in the corner of the room. Bodie Servello's chest tightened with rage.

"Who are you, really?" snapped the Sonoma mayor.

The young man coughed lightly, then removed his cigar from between his lips.

"My name," he said. "Don't tell me you don't know."

"Devil's luck," he muttered.

The young man chuckled in response to the curse.

"My name's Taon Luttrell," he said. "I'm here to deliver some of the tax collection from the village of Sacramento. Take it."

The young man's hand reached into his pocket, searching.

He then hurled something toward Mayor Bodie Servello. The man swiftly dodged and waved his right hand. The object turned out to be roughly a dozen dead scorpions, scattered on the floor. Bodie Servello's wife screamed and fled into the bedroom. The young man's laughter echoed through the room, a jarring and sinister sound that filled the space with unsettling mirth.

Mayor Bodie Servello didn't hesitate. His hand shot out, seizing a spear that hung ominously on the wall.

Armed with the spear, he lunged at the young man with deadly intent. Unfazed, the young man slipped the cigar back between his lips, took a swift drag, and exhaled a plume of smoke straight toward Bodie Servello. The mayor had to sidestep quickly as the cigar smoke, charged with a malevolent energy, swirled toward him like a living thing.

Bodie Servello lunged aggressively from the side, his body coiled with deadly intent. The spear in his hand swung wildly, and his left hand delivered a series of rapid, long-range punches. This technique, typically executed with a sword, demonstrated impressive skill with a spear.

But Bodie Servello was taken aback when the young man, laughing, retorted, "Ah, those fancy moves don't scare me. Bring it on, Bodie Servello."

Despite the attack, the young man stood his ground and countered with an attack of his own.

"Here's the Moonlight Arrow technique, Bodie Servello," the young man declared.

His left arm swung downward in a powerful arc, while his right hand shot up swiftly, almost imperceptibly. Bodie Servello's grip on the spear faltered as his arm clashed with his opponent's. A croaking sound escaped his throat as a strike hit the large vein under his chin. In that instant, his body froze, rigid and unyielding.

Before he was paralyzed, Bodie Servello had grimaced in pain from the blow to his arm, making his expression truly unpleasant to behold. The youth withdrew the cigar from his lips and blew the smoke directly into Bodie Servello's face.

"Well, ain't that a shame," he said. "Your fancy footwork just got schooled by my Moonlight Arrow Opening Move." He blew another puff of cigar smoke into Bodie Servello's face.

The blow to the major nerve beneath Bodie Servello's jaw rendered his body limp, his mouth mute, and his senses dulled. Only his ears remained capable of hearing at that moment.

Then the young man said, "Listen up, Bodie Servello. Tomorrow, Chief Kuiper and the folks from Sacramento are coming. If luck's on your side, they'll take you to the governor in the capital. If not, they'll tear your limb from limb. Before I go, here's a little parting gift from me."

The youth lifted his right index finger.

With the tip of his finger, he drew a dragon on Bodie Servello's forehead.

When Chief Kuiper and two dozen armed residents of Sacramento arrived at the building in Sonoma the next day, they were taken aback to find it abandoned. The structure stood vacant, devoid of any signs of life.

"Damn mayor, you probably skipped town," Kuiper muttered with frustration.

Suddenly, a piercing scream tore through the air from behind the building. As Kuiper and the others hurried around to investigate, they were stunned by the scene before them. Five figures stood motionless inside the horse stable. At the forefront were Mayor Bodie Servello and his wife, flanked by palace guards on either side, with the maid standing behind them. Upon closer inspection, all five were discovered to be alive, their pulses and breaths steady.

Chief Kuiper stared at the dragon emblem etched on Mayor Bodie Servello's forehead. "Dragon," he murmured, shaking his head. "Ladies, ease up. We're bringing Bodie Servello to the capital."

Chapter 11
The Duel in Sonoma Marsh

Dragon Fire Axe Warrior Wintie Rayado moved cautiously toward the riverbank, each step hinting at a lurking threat just beyond view. Finding a secluded spot, he shed his garments and waded into the water, feeling the river's chill wash over him, cleansing not only his body but also the lingering shadows of his past. Amid the bath, he occasionally chuckled, memories of the previous night's Sonoma escapades playing like mischievous phantoms in his mind.

That morning, Kuiper might have already arrived in Sonoma, or he could still be traversing the road, shrouded in the early dawn's shadows. A single malevolent man and his atrocious deeds had met their final reckoning.

The Dragon Warrior knew that, as vast as the world seemed, so was the eternal grip of evil—a force with no end. Emerging from the bath, he felt rejuvenated, as if the waters had cleansed more than just the grime of travel. The sun began its ascent, casting long shadows that stretched and yawned across the land. A whistle escaped his lips as he pondered, his mind retracing the battle with Taon Luttrell and the man who had kidnapped him, challenging him to a confrontation. This memory brought back thoughts of his recent skirmish at the Cave Without a Name with Beretta Wulle.

Once again, he confronted a challenge. Who, he pondered, was the challenger this time? Life weaves a tapestry of challenges—some from within us, others from fellow souls. It was madness, yet within it lay the greatest pleasures. Thus, the Dragon Warrior's whistle soared, weaving an uncertain melody.

Wintie Rayado knew only two details about the man who aided Taon Luttrell's escape. First, under the cover of night, he observed that the man was missing his right arm. Second, when Wintie swung with a third of his might, the man countered with a beam of blue light, thwarting the blow. This indicated that the man, whoever he was, possessed considerable expertise.

The Dragon Warrior speculated that this man could be either Taon Luttrell's mentor or a peer from their school days. After dressing, he resumed his journey.

Wintie Rayado ventured into the treacherous expanse of the Sonoma Marsh, a deadly swampland that devoured anything brave enough to enter its murky depths. Located thirty miles southeast of Sonoma, the region greeted him with fierce northern winds that whipped through his shaggy hair and clothes, causing them to billow and dance.

He glanced down at the wide, marshy plateau, which lay ominously quiet, devoid of any sign of life. Wintie looked up at the sky; the sun silently ascended toward its zenith. From the east, a faint, mocking laughter drifted toward him.

He turned in that direction just as a figure sped across the expansive plateau, moving like an arrow through the gaps in the marshes. As quickly as the laughter had come, it vanished, leaving him beneath the hill where the Dragon Warrior stood. The hill wasn't particularly tall, but from this distance, Wintie Rayado easily recognized the man with the missing arm.

If he's the one who challenged me last night, he must have serious skills and be highly dependable, Wintie Rayado thought to himself. *But,* he added, *how could his skill have improved so drastically in just a few months?*

"The one who goes by Wintie Rayado, the Dragon Fire Axe Warrior, better come down here, or I'll have to come up myself," a male voice echoed from below the hill.

Our warrior let out a sharp whistle.

"If a mouse that's been dining on worms suddenly fancies itself a kitchen cat, things can get messy," he remarked. "So, what's the scoop? You calling me over, kitchen cat?"

Kalin's grim expression grew even darker.

In a loud voice, he retorted, "I figured you didn't have the guts to show up, you crazy warrior. Our little dance from the other day isn't finished yet."

"Well, if that's what this meeting's about, then it's just fine," Wintie said. "Unfinished business needs to be settled, and tangled threads need to be unraveled."

"Spot on," Kalin responded. "But there's one thing, crazy warrior. The Kalin you knew back then isn't the same as the one standing before you today."

Wintie Rayado chuckled. "Well, like I said, you've gone from a mouse with worms to a full-on kitchen cat. But, Kalin, you haven't changed that much. Your arm is still missing, just like before. You ought to find a good woodworker to fashion you a fake one."

Kalin's anger boiled over. His left hand shot up in a swift, upward strike, sending a powerful blast of blue wind hurtling toward Wintie Rayado. The warrior leaped to the side, watching as the ground where he had just stood was obliterated, scattering like a landslide under the force of Kalin's wind strike.

Quietly, Wintie Rayado found himself impressed by his adversary. *Who has Kalin been learning from these past few months?*

"Crazy warrior, quit your boasting and get down here to the marshland," Kalin yelled. "Come down and face your death."

"I don't turn down invitations, whether good or bad, Kalin," Wintie Rayado retorted, then plunged downward like a bird.

As his body floated in the air, Kalin unleashed three consecutive, powerful bare-fisted blows.

The Dragon Warrior countered with a strike from his storm shield that crashed like a tempest upon the ocean. Thus began a fierce clash of mighty blows, each infused with intense internal energy, resulting in thunderous explosions.

For a moment, the Dragon Warrior felt suspended in midair, as if halted by an invisible barrier, while below, Kalin anchored himself firmly into the ground up to his ankles. The Dragon Warrior had not expected such a significant surge in Kalin's internal energy in just a few months.

On the other hand, Kalin grumbled to himself. When he had delivered three consecutive punches earlier, he had expended three-quarters of his internal energy. Despite his exceptional and high-quality martial arts skills, it was clear that his opponent was even more formidable.

Kalin ground his teeth. "You reckless fool, take this blue phantom punch!" he yelled.

His left hand slammed into his face, unleashing a blue beam toward the Dragon Warrior, who had just planted his right foot near the edge of the marsh.

Wintie jumped as high as four spears, delivering a counterblow from that height with equal force. The wind strike resonated like a chorus of hundreds of flutes playing in unison, swirling dust into the air and making the marsh mud appear to boil.

Kalin channeled his internal energy into his legs to defend himself. Though his body trembled under the opponent's wind strike, his legs held firm like steel.

Intrigued, the Dragon Warrior doubled his internal energy for that strike.

Now, Kalin could no longer withstand the full force of the blow. His legs, like tangled roots, tore free from the earth, shattering his defense. His body staggered sharply backward toward the treacherous marsh.

He deflected the opponent's wind strike with a hand against his face, flipping backward over a small marsh in mid-air and landing on another part of the plateau. Now, the two men stood facing each other, separated by the marsh. The man with the missing arm laughed with a cold edge, slipping his left hand behind his clothing.

Moments later, he brandished a blue-colored, stump-bladed sword.

Despite its blade missing, Wintie Rayado recognized, as he gazed at the blue gleam of the sword, that the weapon in his opponent's hand was magical.

"You see this sword, you reckless fool?" hollered Kalin. "Your life hangs by a thread with this weapon."

The Dragon Warrior laughed uproariously. "Folk and his weapon, they're all the same, all equally flawed," jeered Sinforosa Chiflada's disciple.

A deep red flushed across Kalin's face.

"Mocking is easy, but killing you with this weapon will be even easier," Kalin said. "Open your eyes wide, you fool, and take a good look at this." With that, Kalin swept his stump-bladed sword toward the marsh ahead of him.

The marsh mud splattered upward, reaching a height of seven spears. It parted as if cleaved, briefly revealing the dark, murky bottom of the marsh.

What a formidable weapon, Wintie Rayado thought to himself.

Even in this damaged state, it was exceptional.

Imagine its potential in perfect condition.

How did this adversary acquire such a weapon?

"You've seen it, fool," Kalin's voice echoed.

"Your weapon's impressive, Kalin, but rather than using it for ill, it could be better used to forge a replacement arm for you."

Kalin was enraged. He swung the weapon at the Dragon Warrior, unleashing a dazzling blue light.

The Dragon Warrior was no fool. He swiftly channeled his inner energy into both palms and leaped into the air. With a thunderous shout, Wintie Rayado unleashed a barrage of overlapping wind blasts. As the first blast countered Kalin's attack, Wintie followed up with a punch infused with half his full capacity of inner energy. The initial blow halted Kalin's assault, like striking a sheer cliff wall, dispersing the blue light. The second strike not only countered Kalin's attack but also pushed him onto the defensive, forcing him to retreat two spear lengths.

Without hesitation, Wintie surged forward. Kalin's sword slashed fiercely, its blue light sharp and chilling, surging toward the Dragon Warrior.

Wintie Rayado bellowed sharply, causing Kalin's eardrums to tremble. His sword slashed toward his opponent's gut, but in that split second, his foe flickered out of view, disappearing like a ghost in the fog. Frustration simmered in Kalin as he whirled his broken sword in a deadly arc. The twisting, churning blue light wrapped around Wintie Rayado like a malevolent serpent. As the fight intensified, the Dragon Warrior's signature high-pitched whistle cut through the air—a haunting, erratic melody dancing with the chaos. His form became little more than a wraith, flickering in and out of darkness. With his mastery of shadowy martial arts acquired in the shadow cave just days ago, despite only mastering a third of them, Kalin's strikes often found empty space, struggling to discern between Wintie's actual body and mere shadows.

The Dragon Warrior understood that even with twenty techniques, his opponent could not press him, let alone cause him harm. However, it was equally challenging for Wintie to mount a counterattack, as each of Kalin's strikes was a defensive technique. Such was the mastery of the shadowy martial arts possessed by the man with the maimed arm. Yet, it would have been futile for Wintie Rayado to have trained for seventeen years under the powerful Sinforosa Chiflada if he couldn't face such an opponent one-on-one.

The Dragon Fire Axe Warrior swiftly altered his martial arts strategy. He countered Kalin's unexpected moves with his own erratic and unpredictable maneuvers. His hands spread out like the wings of a bird, and a constant, piercing whistle emanated from his mouth, filling Kalin's ears. By then, the two had already clashed thirty times. Remarkably, those thirty moves seemed to pass in the blink of an eye. It was now evident just how severely Kalin was being pressured.

No matter how Kalin quickened his martial arts moves, shifted his tactics, or rampaged like a wounded bull, he couldn't shake off the looming disadvantage. He was now being relentlessly pushed toward the treacherous swamp, each step a dance with death.

"Ha ha ha, it looks like your path to hell leads straight through this deadly swamp, Kalin."

"You worthless scum, stop babbling! Face my demonic stars!" yelled Kalin, leaping forward with his broken sword in hand. With his left hand, he hurled a dozen blue star-shaped objects at his opponent.

"Ah, why bother showing off these kids' toys?" mocked the Dragon Warrior.

His right hand cut through the air in a sweeping arc, generating a whirlwind that dispersed the phantom stars, causing them to miss their mark.

In that instant, as Wintie Rayado reached out to intercept his opponent's hidden weapon, Kalin seized the opportunity to leap across the small marsh.

"Where do you think you're scurrying off to, kitchen cat?" hollered Wintie Rayado.

Kalin hurled a roll of white fabric at the Dragon Warrior.

Initially, Wintie assumed the object was a clandestine weapon, but upon discovering it was merely a rolled-up piece of white paper, he swiftly seized it.

Seizing the moment, Kalin leaped far away, skillfully utilizing his agility to swiftly depart the area.

Wintie had no intention of pursuing the man with the disabled arm. With a mixture of suspicion and intrigue, he carefully unfurled the tightly clasped paper in his hand. It turned out to be a letter from Kalin, addressed directly to him, written in a hurried, almost frantic scrawl.

The scars on my body won't heal. The deaths of my friends and Lyvonte Bicette won't be forgotten as long as I live. You're the root cause of all that. The day of reckoning is coming. If you've got the guts to face what you've done, meet me on the 13th day of the 12th month at the top of Mount Shasta. If you haven't got the nerve to show up, you might as well end it now.

Curiosity gnawed at the Dragon Warrior like a relentless itch.

He crumpled the letter. "Darn kitchen cat," Wintie Rayado grumbled as he sprinted toward the hill.

However, Kalin's shadow had vanished. His challenge in Sonoma Marsh was merely an exploration of how far his supernatural martial arts skills could match his formidable adversary.

In truth, Wintie Rayado remained vastly superior to Kalin.

Yet, he remained undeterred. On that fateful day, his simmering vengeance would come to pass.

And there, in Sonoma Marsh, he had delivered the death invitation letter to his greatest enemy. He was confident that the Dragon Warrior would arrive at the peak of Mount Shasta.

Chapter 12

Echoes of Vengeance on Cerro de las Mitras

The towering peak of Cerro de las Mitras emerged, initially concealed by a veil of white clouds. With the west wind's push, these clouds drifted eastward, gradually revealing the mountain's majestic form in the noonday sun. Moving swiftly, a figure raced toward the summit. As he ascended, the air grew crisper and more invigorating. His pace quickened, driven by an eager anticipation of reaching his destination without delay.

In the time it took to savor a cup of tea, he reached the mountain's pinnacle. Surveying the vista, his gaze swept across a landscape dominated by rocks, ranging from small pebbles to immense boulders resembling houses. Below these slick, moss-draped behemoths, wild grasses flourished. Notably, the man was conspicuously absent an arm.

He stood there as Kalin, unmistakably himself. His sole reason for scaling this mountain peak was to further his grand plan of seeking vengeance upon Dragon Warrior Wintie Rayado.

With a graceful leap, Kalin landed effortlessly on a large rock, a feat beyond the reach of those unaccustomed to controlling their powerful bodies. Attempting such a move would likely result in slipping on the slick moss that covered the rocks.

Kalin surveyed the desolate mountain peak, which was scattered with clusters of rocks. At its heart, a vast dormant crater loomed, its cone-shaped form descending deep into the earth.

Kalin leaped again, this time onto a larger, higher boulder. From this vantage point, he scanned the mountain peak once more. Satisfied that the person he sought was not atop the summit, he swiftly moved to the crater's edge and began his descent into its challenging depths. The crater of Cerro de las Mitras posed formidable obstacles to navigation downward.

But with his nimble agility, Kalin bounded effortlessly from one spot to the next, swiftly reaching the bottom of the crater. The air there was dense and suffocating, weighed down by the mountain's depths.

With a quick adjustment to his breathing, Kalin acclimated to the suffocating air and promptly began to survey the crater's floor beneath him. The expansive base resembled a wide well; its hardened surface was a frozen blend of sand and earth, preserved since the mountain's ancient eruption. Kalin's gaze fixed upon a shoulder-width hole.

Approaching it, he briefly examined the opening before decisively entering without hesitation. Initially confined to crawling, the passage gradually widened as he descended deeper, allowing him to stoop and eventually walk upright.

Kalin arrived at a square room adorned with rough, black stones. Thin wisps of black smoke curled from each of the room's corners, their acrid scent causing Kalin's head to spin suddenly.

Drawing upon his inner strength, Kalin held his breath and quickly scanned the stone room. Though he knew it wasn't a dead end, his eyes found no door or crack.

Looking up, he spotted a stone staircase embedded in the room's ceiling. After a quick survey of the area, he braced his feet and leaped to the edge of the hole, continuing his ascent up the peculiar stone staircase. Despite his skill at lightening his body, each step he took on the staircase echoed loudly through the chamber.

Upon reaching the top step, Kalin stepped into a pristine, immaculate white room where the walls, floor, and ceiling gleamed as if made entirely of glass. In the center of the room, a large stone supported a figure resembling a meditative statue, balanced upside down with legs extended upward and head down. The figure wore a single, tightly wrapped white cloth from calves to chest, and its head and features were obscured beneath a long, floor-length beard that nearly matched cascading hair. It was an unconventional and remarkable pose for meditation. Kalin's attention, however, swiftly shifted upon noticing a large, three-striped tiger lying beside the meditating man, which had caught sight of Kalin's arrival. The majestic creature rose to its feet, growling deeply with its mouth wide open, revealing formidable teeth and dreadfully sharp fangs. With a thunderous roar that shook the room, the tiger leaped forward, claws poised to strike Kalin's flesh.

Kalin, recognizing the tiger as no ordinary beast but the familiar of a sorcerer, swiftly leaped aside to avoid its attack. Yet, despite his speed, the tiger moved with uncanny agility, akin to a seasoned martial arts master. While still airborne, the creature spun mid-air, its tail lashing out like a whip and striking Kalin's shoulder. His clothes tore, and he winced in agonizing pain from the impact.

Summoning his inner strength, Kalin leaped aside once more to evade the tiger's relentless attacks. With swift and agile movements, he deftly dodged each assault, calculating his moves carefully. Despite executing twenty defensive maneuvers, Kalin refrained from retaliating, focusing solely on evasion. The tiger's ferocity threatened to maim him, a reminder of the sorcerer whose familiar it was—a figure Kalin sought to meet and converse with. As the intense struggle unfolded, the meditative figure remained seemingly unperturbed, deep in meditation amid the chaotic skirmish.

Realizing retreat was his sole recourse to avoid injury, Kalin reluctantly exited the white room, biding his time until the meditator finished his contemplation. Just as the tiger roared and prepared to strike again, Kalin swiftly dropped to the floor and rolled toward the stairs. With a quick movement, he disappeared beneath the stairs, evading the tiger's charge.

For three days, Kalin waited patiently at the crater's base.

Three times he had ventured into the white room, observing quietly from behind the top step. Yet the meditator had not budged from his stone. Waiting a week posed no challenge to Kalin, but his concern grew over how to secure food during those four ensuing days of waiting.

On his seventh attempt, Kalin peered cautiously from behind the stairs, only to find the person still deep in meditation. Irritated, Kalin descended once more. As he emerged into the lower room, a sudden echoing sound reverberated from the white room.

"Brave soul who dares to tread with dirty feet upon my land, step forward swiftly to meet your fate."

Kalin was startled to hear this.

"Come quickly! What are you waiting for?" beckoned the voice from the white room.

Kalin retraced his path as he made his way back to the staircase.

The voice echoed again. "Hmm, a one-armed man such as yourself has no place in my domain. Your punishment shall be doubled, human."

Naturally, Kalin was stunned. How could the person in the white room possibly know about his missing arm? Despite wielding extraordinary powers, they had never met in person. It seemed utterly impossible to Kalin that this man could be aware of his missing limb.

Kalin had forgotten that the walls and ceiling of the white room were transparent, allowing those inside to observe anyone below. As he ascended into the white room, to his surprise, the tiger that had previously been aggressive now showed no hostility toward him. Meanwhile, the man draped in white cloth continued to stand with his head resting on the rock, feet raised. Like before, his face remained hidden by a long, flowing white beard, despite the tiger's newfound calmness.

However, Kalin remained vigilant.

"Who are you?" shouted the figure, head down and feet up.

"My name's Kalin. Am I addressing Beda Simplicio?" Kalin asked after introducing himself.

Instead of answering, the person countered with a question: "What brings you to defile my domain, a human with a missing arm?"

"I apologize if my presence here offends your sanctuary; that was never my intention," Kalin replied.

"Enough talk; come closer to receiving your punishment," he declared.

Instead, Kalin stopped in his tracks, observing the man standing on his head atop the rock.

"Step closer," the man commanded.

His voice echoed through the white room, matching the fierce growl of the tiger beside him.

"Beda," Kalin interjected, noticing a slight movement in the man's left foot.

A fierce and relentless gust of wind swept toward Kalin, causing the chamber to quake.

With a swift backflip, Kalin narrowly evaded the ferocious assault. Mocking and cruel laughter filled the air.

"You've got some nerve to come in here and desecrate my domain. It seems you're not without your own skills. Let's see if you can handle my steel leg techniques."

The head atop the rock spun around, and the feet started to shift.

He sensed another imminent strike, a more powerful long-range kick than before. Kalin swiftly advanced and called out, "Beda, wait! I come with news for you."

With that bold proclamation, the man ceased his intention to launch an attack.

"I don't know you. What news do you bring? Speak quickly," he retorted, maintaining his position with his head down and feet up.

"This is bad news, Beda."

"Cursed or blessed, speak quickly. Do not test my patience, ground monkey."

Hearing such venomous words, a flicker of irritation sparked within Kalin, his temper flaring at the crude insults hurled his way.

Despite his irritation, he replied, "Your friend Lyvonte Bicette was killed by some scoundrel."

The figure on the stone stirred, and in an instant, he stood upright, firmly grounded on the stone. His face, previously hidden by the drape of his long white beard, now emerged into view. It was ghostly pale, drained of color, as if blood had long fled. Sunken cheeks and hollow eyes lent a menacing air to his visage. Long white hair cascaded to his shoulders, and his beard flowed down to his stomach.

Kalin bowed respectfully. "So, I am truly face-to-face with Beda Simplicio?" he inquired.

The man with the pale face ignored the question.

"Who killed him, and how do you know?"

Without hesitation, Kalin explained, "Lyvonte Bicette and several other mayors led a contingent of soldiers in battle against Nuevo Reino de León. They were defeated, and Lyvonte Bicette met his end at the hands of a powerful young man."

The creases on Beda Simplicio's face deepened, intensifying his sinister appearance. His eyes narrowed, their gaze sharp as a sword's edge.

He had long been privy to the plan to confront Nuevo Reino de León, as evident from his dealings with Lyvonte Bicette. Driven by a deep-seated vendetta against the royal family, he had pledged to join Bicette's rebellion. Atop Cerro de las Mitras, he awaited updates from Bicette regarding the assault's timing. Today, however, news arrived that the rebellion had faltered and Bicette had perished. Naturally, the revelation was unfathomable.

"I trust not a word you say, you one-armed wretch," growled Beda Simplicio, his voice resonating through the white room.

"Darn it, Beda, I swear I'm not lying," Kalin said calmly, though anger simmered in his heart at being called a one-armed wretch.

"What's your name?"

"Kalin."

"What's your relationship with Lyvonte Bicette?"

"He's been the leader and my close friend for years, Beda."

"Alright, but I'm unsure if it's true. Answer my question to prove your statement. What is Lyvonte Bicette's real name?"

Kalin chuckled softly. "You're quite skeptical of your own people, Beda."

"Who would acknowledge you're on my side with that unappealing face? It's the first time I've seen it."

Kalin muttered under his breath.

"Come on, answer my question. What's Lyvonte Bicette's real name?"

"Supreme!" Kalin replied.

"Hmm," Simplicio mused, "Lyvonte Bicette, a skilled individual, wouldn't meet his end so easily."

"There's always someone stronger, Beda. His rival's skill surpassed his own."

Beda Simplicio frowned, his brow furrowing with concern.

Kalin continued, "I've met him myself. I'm lucky he only took my arm, not my life."

"Ho ho, so you've come here to complain and whine like a child, hoping I'll intervene?"

Kalin blushed. "You see, Beda, as a friend and former leader, I've been searching for the young man who killed Lyvonte Bicette, but he surpasses me in both martial arts and stature."

"What's the bastard's name?" Simplicio demanded.

"Wintie Rayado, but he's better known by the nickname Dragon Fire Axe Warrior."

Upon hearing this, Beda Simplicio was taken aback. "You said he's known as the Dragon Fire Axe Warrior?"

"Yep," Kalin confirmed.

"If that's the case, then she's the old, wrinkled granny, Sinforosa Chiflada."

"No, he's quite young; he looks like a long-haired kid with a twisted, crazy mind."

Simplicio pondered for a moment, then murmured, "If that's true, he might be the pupil of the old woman who resides at the peak of Cerro el Potosí. But as far as I know, Sinforosa Chiflada hasn't had a pupil in decades." He took a deep breath. "If he did indeed learn from Sinforosa Chiflada, it's no wonder Lyvonte Bicette was defeated."

Simplicio's gaze fixed on Kalin's face, as if trying to pierce through the white walls behind him.

Watching closely, Kalin began to sow seeds of doubt. "During our skirmish in the Sonoma Marsh, I warned him that one day Lyvonte Bicette's allies, renowned martial artists, would seek vengeance. Wintie Rayado boasted he feared no one, daring to settle the score at Mount Shasta's summit on the thirteenth day of the twelfth month."

Beda Simplicio's eyes narrowed further.

"Quite arrogant," he muttered. "It seems like he's eager to taste the darkness of the grave, anxious to rush headlong into hell."

"Absolutely, Beda. It's not just his arrogance that stings; his challenge is deeply disrespectful and shows no regard for martial arts figures like yourself."

Simplicio nodded. "People like that need to be dealt with swiftly, or they'll stir up all kinds of trouble for our faction and teachings."

Kalin's heart thumped with glee, knowing his subtle provocations had kindled the flames of Beda's seething rage and deep-seated vendetta.

"That challenge," Kalin continued, stoking the flames, "is also a slap in the face to Lyvonte Bicette's teacher over at Guadalupe Peak. I'm planning to meet with him immediately to figure out our next steps."

"I can handle breaking that loco kid's skull myself."

"Sure, Beda, but to ensure we don't disappoint Lyvonte Bicette's teacher, it would be wise to inform him about his student's death."

"That's up to you," Simplicio replied.

His gaze was fixed squarely on Kalin's waist.

In truth, he had been surreptitiously watching Kalin's waist all along. Suddenly, he said, "I want to see what you're hiding behind your back."

Kalin was taken aback and glanced at his waist. He had hidden his weapon well, but Simplicio's keen eyes had still noticed it. "Ah, it's alright, Beda, just—"

"What do you mean?" Simplicio asked, narrowing his gaze.

"Just an old sword," Kalin replied calmly.

"Bring it out."

"Beda."

"Don't talk too much; just bring it out."

If not for Beda Simplicio standing before him, and if Kalin hadn't been mindful of his greater plan, he might have silenced the man before him. He had sought Simplicio's help, but constant belittlement, insults, curses, and shouts tested his patience.

"You're being defiant, Kalin."

Kalin's curiosity got the better of him, prompting him to unsheathe his enchanted stump sword, filling the room with a sudden blue glow.

Beda Simplicio was taken aback. "The Blue Demon Sword," he muttered. Besides his surprise, he was puzzled to see the once-powerful sword now reduced to a broken piece. "Where did you get that weapon? How did it become broken? Are you a student of the Blue Demon?"

Kalin smirked at the barrage of questions. "That's my concern, Beda. What matters is that we've met today, and you know what happened to Lyvonte Bicette. See you at the top of Mount Shasta." With a shadow-like swiftness, Kalin moved toward the stairs.

"Wait!" shouted Simplicio.

However, Kalin paid no heed.

Enraged, Beda Simplicio declared, "If I didn't think you were once one of Lyvonte Bicette's followers, I might demand your life, Kalin. For now, leave behind one of your earlobes."

A hidden weapon shot toward Kalin's right ear.

He swiftly raised his left hand, but the cursed weapon resisted the internal energy strike. With resignation, Kalin drew his magical sword once more, but it was undoubtedly too late. A groan of pain escaped Kalin as blood dampened his cheek and shoulder. Simplicio's secret weapon had severed his right earlobe.

If not for his focus on revenge, Kalin might have impulsively attacked Beda, especially upon hearing Simplicio's intent to pierce his ear canal. Moments later, Kalin found himself outside the crater of Cerro de las Mitras. He wiped the blood from his cheek, bound his head with a cloth to cover the stump of his ear, and quickly swallowed a pill to counteract the poison from Simplicio's secret weapon.

After Kalin vanished at the base of the Cerro de las Mitras crater, Simplicio found himself deep in contemplation. Kalin's true identity remained shrouded in uncertainty, but that seemed trivial now. What weighed heavily on Simplicio's mind was unraveling the mystery surrounding the youth known as the Dragon Fire Axe Warrior—his connection to Sinforosa Chiflada and whether Kalin had indeed faced him in combat, only to succumb to the young man.

Therefore, Simplicio was compelled to delve deeper into the Dragon Warrior's skill, heightening his eagerness to confront the young warrior promptly. However, he found himself obligated to wait for several months until the appointed day, the thirteenth of the twelfth month.

Chapter 13

The Abduction of Asianna Perlez

Everyone in Pine Springs knew Asianna Perlez. The elderly revered her, the youth adored her, and even the youngest children, tending to their ducks and buffaloes, recognized her presence. Inquiring about Asianna's looks inevitably evoked unanimous admiration.

Indeed, she was unanimously acclaimed as Pine Springs' most beautiful girl. With an oval face, a small, pointed nose reminiscent of a delicate leaf, and lips resembling blooming pomegranates—red and fresh—Asianna captivated all who beheld her. Her eyes sparkled like stars, her chin was delicate as a hanging bee, and her slender neck added to her graceful allure. Her voice was soft and melodious, a soothing delight to the ear. Her plump, firm body was adorned with smooth, soft skin, completing her radiant presence.

Asianna Perlez lived up to every bit of her reputation for stunning beauty. Her presence stirred envy among the girls of Pine Springs and left many young men hopelessly smitten. However, their admiration would soon turn to disappointment, as next month, under the fourteen-day-old moon, Asianna Perlez was set to marry Ranger, the son of the village head.

Ranger wasn't just wealthy, with expansive fields and abundant cattle; he was a perfect match for Asianna Perlez. Handsome and robust, with a genuine heart and a warm demeanor, he complemented

Asianna perfectly. As their wedding day neared, anticipation mounted, and the atmosphere became laden with significance. It wasn't merely a day—it was a moment destined to be etched in their memories forever, a day when they would embark together on the journey to uncover the secrets of happiness.

Ranger sat on his porch, his gaze fixed on the stars above. That night, an unsettling feeling gnawed at his heart—an inexplicable sense of foreboding that lingered, refusing to dissipate despite his efforts to pinpoint its source.

He only managed to drift off to sleep in the late hours of the night. However, just before dawn, he jolted awake with a start. Ranger, who had honed his skills in martial arts and mysticism under a master from the northern coast, felt a prickling of instinct—a chilling certainty that someone else was in his room. As he opened his eyes, he was stunned to find a diminutive figure standing near his bed. The creature's bald head gleamed under the flickering lamplight, casting an eerie glow on its shiny scalp. Its disproportionately large nose nearly obscured its small, grinning face, and in that grin, a single upper tooth glinted in the dimness.

Ranger leaped out of bed, his voice ringing out, "Hey, you there! Who are you?"

His gaze bore into the figure before him, sharp and searching.

Despite the dim glow of the oil lamp, Ranger could discern that the short figure had unusually large and wide feet, resembling those of an elephant.

"Hehehe," chuckled the short man. "Are you Ranger, the one getting married next week?"

Naturally, this question caught Ranger by surprise.

"That's none of your concern! Now, who in blazes are you?"

"Hehehe..." The uninvited guest chuckled again. "You'll never marry Asianna Perlez, Ranger!"

"Don't you go talking nonsense in the middle of the night, shorty!" Ranger shouted angrily. "Get out of my room!" He clenched his fists tightly.

"You'll never lay a finger on Asianna Perlez, young man. From now on, she's mine. I'll take her wherever I want and do as I please!" The short man chuckled once more.

"If you want to rant, do it in your grave!" Ranger lunged forward, his right fist aimed at the intruder, but he struck nothing.

The short man moved with such lightning speed that he vanished in an instant.

Left alone in the room, Ranger felt as if he had been abruptly awakened from a dream. He rubbed his eyes repeatedly. No, he wasn't dreaming! He was certain of it. Glancing down at the wooden floor, he noticed the distinct footprints left by the short man. Recalling the intruder's ominous words, a sense of unease gnawed at him.

He seized a pointed iron staff hanging on the wall, a gift from his teacher. Without hesitation, he left his house and headed toward the eastern village, where Asianna Perlez's parents resided. As he neared, just ten yards from his fiancée's front yard, Ranger caught sight of a figure leaping from a side window—the same short man who had visited him earlier. The man was carrying a female figure draped over his shoulder.

Despite the darkness, Ranger recognized his fiancée, Asianna Perlez. "You scoundrel! Thief! Release that woman!" Ranger shouted.

The bald-headed man laughed coldly. "Once she's mine, no one can stop me!"

"If that's how it's going to be, I'll crack your skull!"

Ranger swung his iron staff toward the short man's head, but the target swiftly leaped aside. Undeterred, Ranger followed with a stab aimed at the man's left chest, but the short man moved with astonishing speed, kicking Ranger's right hand. The iron staff flew from his grip, and pain shot through his crushed hand, prompting him to scream in agony.

Ranger staggered and collapsed several yards away from the force of the short man's kick to his stomach, his abdomen torn open. He lay motionless on the ground. The short man cackled with malevolence.

"You low-down thief! Your life is about to end with my blade!" someone shouted, leaping from the window.

The bald-headed short man swiftly turned as a machete swung toward his head.

"Hey... You want to join the dead, mountain folk?" said the short man.

The assailant turned out to be Tanqueray, Asianna Perlez's father.

"You'll be the first to perish, cursed soul!"

Tanqueray's machete slashed again, but the short man proved to be remarkably agile.

He faced the attack with a sneer, swiftly incapacitating Tanqueray with a single, decisive move. The short man chuckled triumphantly.

"Both the future son-in-law and the father-in-law are out of luck! Such a shame," he remarked before taking a deep breath of the morning air and disappearing from sight.

When the bald-headed man reached his hermitage atop Guadalupe Peak, a sudden unease gripped him. Standing by the door was an unexpected stranger—a one-handed man whose presence unsettled him deeply. Likewise, the one-handed man seemed equally surprised to see the bald-headed man, who arrived with a beautiful girl draped over his shoulder.

He quickly bowed and exclaimed, "Well, I'll be! Am I in the presence of the renowned martial artist known as Elephant Foot?"

Elephant Foot, the bald-headed man, gently lowered Asianna Perlez from his shoulder. His keen eyes fixed on the stranger as he inquired, "Who are you? Do you come with good intentions or bad?" During their exchange, Elephant Foot couldn't ignore the stranger's mangled and misshapen right ear.

"My name is Kalin. I mean no harm, but I bring troubling news."

"I don't know you. What troubling news do you bring?" Elephant Foot asked.

So Kalin quickly got to the point. "The murder of a disciple is a bitter pill for his master to swallow—so bitter that it stirs deep-seated vengeance."

"Cut the riddles!" Elephant Foot interrupted. "Just tell me straight!"

"Your disciple has been murdered, Elephant Foot."

The bald-headed man's face contorted, displaying a range of emotions.

Meanwhile, Kalin glanced at Asianna Perlez, who stood motionless, seemingly petrified. *Who is this beautiful girl?* Kalin wondered in his heart, struck by Asianna Perlez's captivating beauty.

"I've got disciples who've ventured into the martial forest. Which one are you talking about?" Elephant Foot demanded.

Kalin turned back to the man. "Lyvonte Bicette."

"I ain't got no disciple named Lyvonte Bicette!" Elephant Foot declared.

Kalin was taken aback. After a moment's pause, he recollected, "I mean your disciple, Supreme."

Once again, Elephant Foot's expression shifted, suspicion stirring within him.

"Are you speaking the truth?"

"By Satan and his demons, I swear I'm not lying, Elephant Foot!"

"Supreme isn't an ordinary man. His martial arts skills are top-notch!"

"But the person who did him in is even more skilled!"

"Who did it?"

"Dragon Warrior did it."

Elephant Foot mulled it over, his fists tightening. "You're lying! Dragon Warrior Sinforosa Chiflada vanished from the martial world decades ago!"

"But—"

"Shut up! Take your punishment, you lying bastard!" Elephant Foot yelled, lashing out and kicking him in the face.

The wind, as fierce as a storm unleashed by Elephant Foot's kick, struck Kalin before he could retaliate.

Kalin didn't dare take chances. He shouted loudly and leaped eight feet into the air. Glancing back, his throat tightened as he saw Elephant Foot's kick shatter a large rock behind him with the force of the wind.

Just as the man was preparing for another strike, Kalin hastily shouted, "Hold up! We're on the same side!"

Elephant Foot retracted his attack. "What do you mean we're on the same side, huh?"

"I used to work under Supreme back in Dimmitt!"

"Don't try to fool me!" Elephant Foot snapped.

"Why would I gain anything from lying to you?" Kalin retorted defiantly.

"Show me proof that my disciple was really murdered!"

Kalin chuckled coldly. "Stubborn disbelief will only harm you, Elephant Foot." Then, Kalin proceeded to provide more details.

Now, Elephant Foot's face began to show signs of trust, but Kalin's mention of Dragon Warrior Wintie Rayado raised new doubts.

Elephant Foot concluded logically that Wintie Rayado must have been a disciple of Sinforosa Chiflada. "The black faction has always harbored a vendetta against that cursed old woman," Elephant Foot said. "Just as we were ready to eliminate her, she vanished! Now her disciple shows up and takes out mine! It's a damn curse!"

"I faced him in Sonoma Marsh to avenge Supreme or Lyvonte Bicette's deaths. That kid's got skills, though. Losing the fight in Sonoma Marsh isn't the worst part—what really eats at me, Elephant Foot..."

Kalin's face contorted with vengeance, and his eyes locked on the distant horizon.

"Share with me what's troubling you!" Elephant Foot demanded.

"Before I left Sonoma Marsh, I warned that kid that Supreme's master's revenge was coming! He just laughed and said, Even if there were a thousand teachers like Supreme, he'd flatten them all!"

Elephant Foot's jaw clenched tightly.

"That's what the damn bastard said?"

Kalin nodded.

"Even though he's Sinforosa Chiflada's disciple, he's not invincible! Where's that damn bastard? I, Elephant Foot, will crush him!"

"No need to go hunting, Elephant Foot," Kalin replied. "Remember what I told you? He was just taunting you. He said he'd be waiting for you on the thirteenth day of the twelfth month at the peak of Mount Shasta!"

"That lowlife!" Elephant Foot spat on the ground.

Kalin added, "I've also notified several top martial arts figures who were challenged by Dragon Warrior. They've agreed to come to Mount Shasta to settle things with him!"

"Let a thousand come if they want. But that scum's fate will be decided by me!"

Kalin nodded, satisfied. This was exactly what he had hoped for.

Alone, he couldn't take on Wintie Rayado. But with Elephant Foot, Beda Simplicio, Willman, and Taon Luttrell strategizing together, not even three Dragon Warriors could match them.

"I'm glad you're on board, Elephant Foot. I'll definitely be at the peak of Mount Shasta."

Elephant Foot chuckled coldly. "If you're brave but lacking in wisdom, you'd best stay away!"

Kalin's face flushed with anger.

"Now I have no business with you! Get outta here!" Elephant Foot snapped.

Kalin glanced at Asianna Perlez, then faced Elephant Foot squarely. "Don't underestimate me, Elephant Foot. I may not be famous in the martial arts world, but I can still shatter a rock like the one earlier." Kalin rested his hand on his waist.

Suddenly, a beam of blue light streaked toward the large rock, about nine paces away. The rock shattered into pieces, and Kalin's silhouette vanished immediately after.

Elephant Foot was taken aback. He hadn't anticipated that a one-handed man like Kalin could possess such skill. However, the bald man didn't dwell on it for long.

The moment Elephant Foot laid eyes on Asianna Perlez's face and figure, everything else faded from his mind.

Without hesitation, he led the girl into the hermitage. What transpired between him and the innocent girl afterward remained a mystery. But that day, innocence was lost, consumed by darkness.

Chapter 14

The Convergence on Mount Shasta

Atop Mount Shasta's peak, on the thirteenth day of the twelfth month, the fierce north wind dominated over its gentler western counterpart. The summit lay shrouded in profound silence, as if anticipating the arrival of human ambition. Amid the dense fir trees that stood sentinel just yards from the crater's edge, their towering forms swaying in the vigorous north wind, thin smoke tinged with sulfur endlessly billowed from the wide crater. The morning sun, positioned precisely between zenith and ascent, cast its light anew. Amid the rustling of fir leaves, a haunting whistle echoed across Mount Shasta's peak, reverberating through the collapsed crater and swirling sulfur mist. Its irregular, uncertain notes wove an enchanting melody that transported listeners to fantastical realms. Yet, nearing noon, the solitary figure who produced the whistle remained alone—the tallest fir tree marked the presence of Wintie Rayado, the Dragon Fire Axe Warrior. His ascent had been spurred by a challenge from his old foe, Kalin, but atop this peak, unexpected encounters awaited—renowned martial artists poised for challenge.

Wintie whistled intermittently, his eyes scanning the expanse of the mountain peak, where silence and tranquility reigned. He surveyed the base and slopes, all cloaked in stillness and peace. After a few sips of tea, Wintie's keen, well-honed ears faintly detected a sound.

He immediately stopped whistling and turned his head eastward toward the source of the sound. Though still out of sight, the noise grew louder. Moments later, a head emerged from behind a rocky mound at the crater's eastern edge, followed by a chest, and then a full figure. This was not Kalin—his right arm was intact.

Think you're getting one thing; end up with another, Wintie Rayado muttered to himself.

His eyes remained fixed on the newcomer, who seemed to be scanning the area, possibly searching for someone. The newcomer was an old man.

Wintie guessed he was at least fifty, but despite his age, his frame was sturdy. A golden dagger gleamed at his waist.

From his calm and graceful movements, Wintie knew this old man had to be a high-level martial arts master. *Maybe he lives around Mount Shasta, or perhaps he just happened to show up on the day I'm set to face Kalin,* the Dragon Warrior thought to himself.

Meanwhile, the unfamiliar old man stood at the crater's edge, peering down before turning to survey the entire mountain with his small, sharp eyes.

Eventually, he strolled over to the row of fir trees and settled down to rest.

Wintie realized the elderly man had come to this place in search of someone, and having found no one, he opted to wait instead. With no sense of kinship toward him, Wintie remained perched atop his lofty fir tree as the sun climbed higher toward noon, keeping his gaze fixed on the elderly man. Suddenly, the man turned southward. A figure darted past, arriving without Wintie hearing or sensing him—an impressive display of speed and agility. What intrigued the Dragon Warrior was that this person was not Kalin, whom he awaited. The newcomer was stout, with a bald head gleaming in the sunlight and feet as wide and thick as an elephant's.

Suddenly, the Dragon Warrior recalled his teacher's words. According to her, atop Guadalupe Peak resided a renowned martial artist known as Elephant Foot, named for his feet, which resembled those of an elephant and were integral to his remarkable skill.

He could shatter even a stone with a kick.

And right then, Wintie noticed how the ground under the man's feet sank deep into the mountain soil. *Maybe this fella's Elephant Foot,* mused Wintie Rayado. *But what's he doing here?* Just as he pondered this, Wintie was taken aback to see the old man under the fir tree suddenly stand tall to greet the arrival of the short man.

Their eyes met in an instant. With a swift leap, the short man closed the distance, standing just two spear-lengths away from the old man with the dagger. Once more, they locked gazes, sizing each other up.

Then, the short man's voice echoed out, "Well, look who's here first, that wild warrior Wintie Rayado? It seems like you're just itching for a quick death!"

The outburst of anger caused Elephant Foot to momentarily forget Kalin's information that Wintie Rayado was a young man. Both the old man, looking shocked and surprised, and the Dragon Warrior, perched in the fir tree, furrowed their brows at the short man's shout.

Before the old man could say a word, the short man hollered, "What a death wish you've got, Dragon Warrior! I'm Elephant Foot, and I'll make it happen right now!"

"If I'm facing Elephant Foot, the famous martial artist from Guadalupe Peak, right now," the old man replied, "then you're dead wrong!"

Elephant Foot's eyes widened in surprise.

"Wrong? What do you mean?" He recalled Kalin's information, then queried, "Aren't you Wintie Rayado, that fool they call the Dragon Warrior?"

The old man shook his head solemnly.

"I'm Willman, Head of the White Lotus School on Cerro de la Silla," he stated firmly.

"Well, well… I didn't reckon I'd run into a renowned martial artist from afar," Elephant Foot said warmly. Recalling that Willman hailed from the white faction while he belonged to the black, Elephant Foot inquired, "What's got the Head of the White Lotus School out here?"

"The tale's a long one, Elephant Foot," replied the old man with the dagger. "In brief, I'm here to seek out and answer the call of a rogue named Wintie Rayado, who goes by the name Dragon Warrior!"

"Well, well, well! If that's the case, we both came here for the same reason. And surely we share the same end goal: to put an end to that cursed man's life. Ain't that right?"

Though taken aback by Elephant Foot's knowledge, Willman nodded in solemn agreement.

"Same purpose, same end goal, but our backgrounds sure differ. If you don't mind me asking, Why did the Head of the White Lotus School come personally instead of sending his disciples?"

"All my disciples were taken out by that cursed man! Two of them were violated," replied Willman, his voice shaking. Then he recounted the tragic events involving the school and his disciples.

Perched in the fir tree, Dragon Warrior Wintie Rayado strained to hear every word, his eyes widening at Willman's shocking account. Since descending the mountain, he had never heard of the White Lotus School, nor had he met Willman before today. Yet, here was the school's head accusing him of slaughtering his disciples en masse—a blatant falsehood. If it wasn't a mistake, it was slander. And if not slander, what had convinced Willman that Dragon Warrior was responsible for the school's destruction?

"Seems like our fates ain't too different, White Lotus Head," Elephant Foot's voice rang out. "That fool killed my disciple, Supreme!"

Now it all made sense to Wintie Rayado.

Elephant Foot seemed to be the master of Supreme, also known as Lyvonte Bicette.

"He only took out one of your disciples, but mine... he wiped them all out," Willman replied.

"The count doesn't matter, White Lotus Head. What matters is that fool's a degenerate who needs to be erased from this earth."

Willman nodded in agreement.

Elephant Foot was about to speak again but halted as he caught sight, out of the corner of his eye, of a figure darting and suddenly appearing before them.

Who else is coming now? Wintie Rayado mused.

Elephant Foot exclaimed in surprise, "Well, ain't this a surprise? How'd a martial artist from Cerro de las Mitras end up here?"

The newcomer chuckled heartily. Dressed in white clothing, his long hair cascaded like a woman's, and his beard extended down to his stomach. Both hair and beard were white, dancing in the wind.

"Why are you lounging around here?" The old man with the white beard shot back, glancing over at Willman.

Elephant Foot introduced Willman to the white-bearded man, who turned out to be Beda Simplicio, a formidable figure from Cerro de las Mitras.

After hearing Elephant Foot's account, which also included Willman's story, Beda Simplicio took a deep breath and remarked, "It's truly unexpected that all three of us have converged here with the same intent! I knew Lyvonte Bicette well. I had pledged to assist him in bringing down Nuevo Reino de León, as I've harbored a longstanding grudge against that kingdom. But it seems Lyvonte beat me to the punch! One of his men informed me. Apparently, before the conflict erupted, Lyvonte dispatched a messenger. Unfortunately, Nuevo Reino de León's patrols intercepted the messenger!"

A brief silence fell over them.

Perched atop the fir tree, Wintie Rayado remained motionless. As the three men arrived and shared their tales, Wintie began to feel a sense of unease. The focus of this disturbance seemed to be directed at him. It didn't take much to figure out who might be behind this—Kalin. But where was Kalin?

Certain that more than just these three would show up, Wintie chose to bide his time. His hunch was spot on. Just over a cup of tea later, two figures dashed in from the west like the wind. One, with a mutilated arm, was instantly recognized by Wintie Rayado as Kalin. The other figure gave the Dragon Warrior pause.

Recognizing the dragon tattoo on his forehead, Wintie recalled him as Taon Luttrell, leader of the Black Trio from Río Colorado, who had clashed with him before but had been saved by Kalin later on. As they approached Elephant Foot, Willman, and Beda Simplicio, both men immediately bowed.

Kalin looked around at their surroundings. "Pardon our tardiness," he said, scanning the area once more.

All the invited individuals had finally arrived.

"That crazy warrior isn't here yet!"

Taon Luttrell cleared his throat. "I reckon that cowardly boy won't dare to show his face here!"

"If he's up for the challenge, he'll show up," Kalin shot back.

"Let's hold off for now," Beda Simplicio suggested.

"And even if that cursed one doesn't appear, I'll chase him down to hell's gates!" declared the Head of the White Lotus School.

Kalin's satisfaction was evident upon hearing Willman's words. It was clear the elderly man harbored a deep resentment toward Wintie Rayado.

Meanwhile, perched atop the fir tree, Dragon Warrior Wintie Rayado watched intently below. It was clear now that Kalin had orchestrated the presence of these three top martial artists. Five individuals awaited him.

Wintie had assessed Kalin's and Taon Luttrell's abilities, but what about the other three? Could he confront all five of them simultaneously?

The Dragon Warrior silently drew a deep breath, gazing up at the sky where the sun had reached its zenith. Should he make his presence known now or wait for the opportune moment?

At that moment, from below, Elephant Foot's voice carried, "I ain't convinced that kid's truly Sinforosa Chiflada's disciple. That old lady left the martial world long ago."

Wintie Rayado's heart stirred at his words, spoken in such a manner. No longer hesitating, driven by instinct, a whistle escaped his lips. The five individuals beneath the fir tree startled, looking up.

"Outrageous! It seems that bold kid's been up there all along!" cursed Kalin.

"Mad warrior, descend and face your fate!" shouted Willman.

The Dragon Warrior chuckled. "Head of the White Lotus School, you're pitiful! Unaware that you've been deceived by that mutilated arm!"

Kalin snapped quickly. "It looks like you've chosen death up there on that tree, Wintie Rayado? That tree's tall enough to send your sorry soul straight to hell!"

Wintie chuckled once more, as he had done before.

"I'll make him come down!" declared Taon Luttrell.

His right hand darted, launching three deadly flying daggers toward the summit of the fir tree where the Dragon Warrior perched.

"Taon Luttrell! If you're as skilled as you claim, why not come and reclaim your daggers?" Wintie shouted down from the treetop.

Just as the words escaped his lips, a fierce wind erupted. In a chilling display of malevolent precision, three daggers sliced through the air, hurtling back toward their bewildered owner with lethal intent.

Taon Luttrell twisted and contorted, narrowly evading the first two daggers with desperate agility. Yet the third dagger surged with relentless, almost supernatural speed, homing in on his head like a predatory bird of prey. Beda Simplicio's shout came just in time. With a casual flick of his hand, the dagger veered off course, narrowly sparing Taon Luttrell from a deadly strike.

Taon Luttrell felt a chill race across his skin, thankful to evade death's icy grasp.

Wintie Rayado chuckled deeply. "You're too foolish to be out here, Taon Luttrell! You should've been washing up and hitting the sack by now."

In that instant, Willman's patience reached its breaking point.

He brought his right hand down hard against the trunk of a fir tree, causing it to topple with a thunderous crash.

Wintie leaped aside, landing smoothly. As he descended, he quipped, "There was only one challenger. Why are there five now? Can you multiply, Kalin?" Then, turning to the three martial arts masters, Wintie shouted, "You old fools are still entangled in worldly affairs and bloodlust! Aren't you ashamed to be provoked by that one-armed monkey?"

"Enough of your yammering, you daft fool! Your time's up!" Elephant Foot shouted, stepping in and delivering a right kick before Dragon Warrior even touched down.

The force of his kick was staggering, sending dust billowing into the air.

To gauge his opponent's resolve, Wintie deliberately chose not to dodge, opting instead to counter with a punch.

When their forces collided, Elephant Foot was taken aback as his feet sank three inches into the ground. His powerful kick, which was capable of shattering stones, was completely nullified. It became clear that the Dragon Warrior possessed formidable inner strength.

With two effortless somersaults, Wintie landed gracefully on his feet, instantly surrounded by the five men. "You old coots, ain't you ashamed to gang up like this?" Dragon Warrior taunted with a smirk.

"A scraggly mutt like you deserves to be put down!" Willman shot back.

"Ah, old man," Wintie drawled, "seems like you've been misled. I swear, I never set foot in your school. Whatever happened there ain't my doing—it's all lies. Someone else is behind it. I reckon it's that one-armed fella!" Wintie jabbed a finger toward Kalin.

"Hahaha! It's not time to wash your hands of this yet, wild warrior!" Kalin chuckled, twirling his broken sword in his left hand. "No need to point fingers or spread falsehoods!"

"I ain't accusing you, one-armed man. But if you look in Beda Simplicio's mirror, you might just see a goat staring back!"

Kalin's face flushed crimson with anger.

Wintie chuckled heartily, his laughter booming through the air.

Feeling insulted, Beda Simplicio stepped forward. "Enough talk, amigos! Let's deal with this fool!" he declared, waving his hand emphatically.

A searing, blinding white light shot toward Wintie's face. The instant it struck his eyes, Dragon Warrior's vision plunged into darkness.

"Damn!" Wintie swore under his breath. Gathering his focus, he swiftly leaped toward one of the fir trees for cover.

Elephant Foot didn't stay idle, launching relentless kicks. The fir tree shattered under the assault, but Wintie had already evaded him.

With his eyes shut, he whirled his arms in the air, conjuring a hurricane-like barrier. Even with just a fraction of his inner strength, the force of the attack was sufficient to scatter his five assailants. As he reopened his eyes, clarity returned to his vision.

Beda Simplicio was stunned to see that his opponent's eyes remained unaffected by the glare from the mirror.

Meanwhile, Wintie recognized the threat posed by Beda Simplicio's mirror, considering it the most dangerous weapon among his attackers. He made it his priority to destroy it first, but being surrounded by five foes made this a daunting task. The assaults were relentless; every attempt to shatter Beda Simplicio's mirror was met with Kalin's sword, Taon Luttrell's machete, and Elephant Foot's kicks all at once.

Swiftly maneuvering and countering with his bare hands, the Dragon Warrior held his ground through twelve exchanges. As the onslaught intensified with each subsequent move, he began to feel the strain. The large machete slashed repeatedly at his chest and stomach, Kalin's sword's blue glow sliced through his defenses, and Willman's golden dagger jabbed at him mercilessly. Amid the chaos, Elephant Foot's relentless kicks and Beda Simplicio's mirror incessantly targeted his face, narrowly evading each strike. By the fifteenth exchange, Sinforosa Chiflada's student found himself cornered at the edge of the crater. The mirror's light flashed toward his face as Elephant Foot's kick aimed for his groin. From above, the Blue Demon Sword descended with a roar, the golden dagger struck at his chest, and Taon Luttrell's machete sliced across his abdomen.

"Your time's almost up, you wild kid!" Kalin shouted.

"Don't forget to give my regards to the demons in hell!" Willman added with a sneer.

The tip of the Blue Demon Sword slashed across his chest, tearing Dragon Warrior's clothing apart.

"Damn it!" Wintie swore under his breath.

"Go ahead and curse, forest demon! The demons of hell love foul-mouthed men like you!" Kalin shouted tauntingly.

Wintie clenched his teeth, his cheeks swelling with pent-up rage. Moments later, he unleashed a deafening roar that echoed through

Mount Shasta's crater. In an instant, Dragon Warrior vanished. Simultaneously, a high-pitched whistle pierced the air, accompanied by a sound like hundreds of bees buzzing. White light swirled around him, causing the five attackers to instinctively step back.

"Dragon Fire Axe!" Beda Simplicio exclaimed as he noticed the weapon in Wintie's hand.

Before the echo of his shout faded, a piercing scream tore through the air. Taon Luttrell's body thudded to the ground, blood-soaked, and his head split in two—the first victim of the Dragon Fire Axe.

"Surround him tightly!" Elephant Foot shouted, leaping high into the air.

Both his feet lashed out in quick succession, while the other two weapons hurtled toward Wintie Rayado with a menacing speed.

"Leader of the White Lotus School!" Dragon Warrior called out. "I have no quarrel with you. You should step back!"

"Quit talking nonsense, wild youth! The spirits of my eight disciples cry out for your wretched soul," Willman snarled, thrusting his dagger faster.

The clash of the golden dagger, Blue Demon Sword, and Dragon Fire Axe reverberated loudly.

Willman exclaimed in surprise, his hand trembling violently from the searing heat. His sacred dagger slipped from his grasp, soaring out of reach. The leader of the White Lotus School swiftly leaped backward.

Kalin was equally taken aback. The jagged edge of his shattered sword was nicked, his hand feeling rigid. If not for Beda Simplicio's mirror flashing light at their opponent, Dragon Fire Axe would have cleaved into his stomach.

Kalin broke out in a cold sweat as the Dragon Warrior's whistle was occasionally interrupted by mocking laughter. His body seemed almost ethereal as the Dragon Fire Axe thirsted for blood. The four opponents were fully engaged.

Sensing he was trapped, Elephant Foot swiftly reached into his pocket. Suddenly, the martial arts master unleashed a hundred black needles at Wintie Rayado. However, the powerful wind from the Dragon Fire Axe deflected the toxic barrage. Elephant Foot and his comrades had to quickly dodge the rebounding needles instead.

"Hehehe..." Dragon Warrior chuckled mockingly. "Willman, consider this your final warning. Back off or face your end!"

The leader of the White Lotus School hesitated.

He wondered, *Is there truly such a formidable foe giving me two warnings?*

"Don't be a fool, Willman!" Kalin shouted. "You want to let the man who killed your eight disciples go—ah..."

Kalin's words were abruptly silenced as one of the blades of Wintie Rayado's Dragon Fire Axe sliced through his left arm. His arm and the broken sword tumbled into the crater below, blood spraying forth as Kalin staggered back, overcome with agony.

As his life ebbed away, he lay on the ground, still breathing but fading fast. Elephant Foot and Beda Simplicio were momentarily stunned, then launched into a fierce assault. Their efforts were met with mocking laughter and whistling from Wintie Rayado.

"You two are practitioners of dark sorcery! People like you belong in hell, feeding worms!" The Dragon Warrior spun his axe menacingly.

The mirror wielded by Beda Simplicio shattered into countless pieces.

Beda Simplicio stifled a cry, staring in disbelief at his shattered weapon.

"Beda, watch out!" Elephant Foot exclaimed urgently.

But it was too late! The Dragon Fire Axe swung at him without mercy or a chance to evade. Beda Simplicio's neck was severed, blood spraying into the air as his head rolled like a ball into Mount Shasta's crater.

Witnessing his friend's death, Elephant Foot, typically so brave, faltered in courage and, without hesitation, turned and fled.

"Hey, shorty, where do you think you're going?" Wintie Rayado shouted. "Stop right there!"

However, Elephant Foot had no intention of stopping. He sprinted as swiftly as he could.

Wintie grinned wickedly as he pressed a part near the handle of the dragon-shaped axe. Two hundred and twelve deadly white needles shot toward Elephant Foot.

Elephant Foot tried to dodge, but he wasn't fast enough; almost all the needles pierced his flesh. He bellowed in agony as the poison reached his heart, his body convulsing violently before slumping lifeless to the ground.

Willman marveled at Dragon Warrior's skill, though secretly, fear raised the hairs on his neck. When he glanced back at the young warrior, he saw Wintie Rayado standing there, casually scratching his long hair.

Wintie took a deep breath, turned to face Willman, and began to speak. "Leader of the White Lotus School," he started calmly, "the truth can be unbelievable until witnessed firsthand, much like what occurred at your school. I had no part in those events. I believe this man is the true culprit." Wintie then walked toward the gasping Kalin, pulling a pill from his pocket and twirling it with a smile. "Do you still wish to live, Kalin?" he asked.

Kalin remained silent.

"This pill can heal your wounds and neutralize the Dragon Fire Axe poison in your bloodstream. I'll give it to you if you confess to the murder of the eight students of the White Lotus School."

Kalin stayed silent.

"Don't you want to survive?"

Kalin's eyes gleamed as he stared at the pill in Wintie's hand. In every dying soul, there lingered a flicker of hope for survival.

Kalin was no different. "Give me the pill first," he demanded.

Wintie slipped the pill into Kalin's mouth, and Kalin swallowed it quickly. "Now, explain quickly!"

Kalin began to confess his actions to the White Lotus School.

Upon hearing this, Willman erupted in fury. Without a moment's hesitation, he delivered a powerful kick with his right foot. The force of the blow sent Kalin's body soaring several yards into the air before tragically plunging into the crater below. Kalin's scream reverberated as he plummeted into the sulfur pit.

Once more, Dragon Warrior took a deep breath and turned to face Willman. A grin spread across the young warrior's face, and the leader of the White Lotus School responded with a faint smile.

"Young man, are you really a student of Sinforosa Chiflada?"

"Ah, it doesn't matter whose student I am, leader of the White Lotus School," Dragon Warrior replied. "People call me crazy, insane, or mad. But sometimes, madness has its purpose. Only madmen like us can eliminate wickedness and destroy evil. Consider this: Would any sane person want to take another human's life?"

Willman chuckled. "You're right, warrior," he said.

Wintie looked up at the sky. "Ah, the sun is high. Many new tasks await us. Leader of the White Lotus School, our meeting ends here. It's been good meeting you. I hope our paths cross again."

"Dragon Warrior, wait," called Willman.

But it was in vain. The young warrior had vanished without a trace.

Willman shook his head. "He's an extraordinary young man. He seems quite mad, but with a pure heart and skills... Oh, I, an old man, may never attain his level of expertise. Before I could even express my gratitude, he vanished." Willman glanced at the crater, then followed Wintie Rayado's path, departing from the scene.

Don't miss out!

Visit the website below and you can sign up to receive emails whenever Frank Spreader publishes a new book. There's no charge and no obligation.

https://books2read.com/r/B-A-QABKB-KCIRD

BOOKS 2 READ

Connecting independent readers to independent writers.

Did you love *The Vengeance of the Mighty*? Then you should read *Echoes of the Cuchillo*[1] by Frank Spreader!

In the heart of the Spanish Empire's zenith, La Florida is plunged into chaos as treacherous rebels seize power, igniting a brutal conflict for control. Amid the bloodshed, the skilled leader Braison Pakenham faces a devastating defeat at the hands of the formidable Sindarius Irelands. As the grand vizier falls and the governor narrowly escapes with the sacred Cuchillo del Sol Naciente, hope seems all but lost.

Enter the enigmatic Dragon Warrior, Wintie Rayado, whose unparalleled skills and unyielding resolve offer a glimmer of hope. In a series of fierce confrontations against the rebels and the dark Soul Reaping Demons, Wintie, alongside the mysterious Blue Hooded

---

1. https://books2read.com/u/bM0XR5

2. https://books2read.com/u/bM0XR5

Deity, fights to protect the sacred dagger and restore order. As alliances shift and betrayals unravel, the fate of La Florida hangs in the balance.

With epic battles, hidden agendas, and a relentless quest for vengeance, "Echoes of the Cuchillo" is a gripping tale of honor, sacrifice, and the fight for redemption in a land where every victory comes at a steep price.

Also by Frank Spreader

The Dragon Warrior
The Vengeance of the Mighty
Echoes of the Cuchillo

Standalone
Fond Memory in Indian Rocks Beach
Piece of Life: Undeserved Maid
Piece of Life: Adolescent Adventure
Piece of Life: Dramatic Karma
Piece of Life: Back to Hometown pt. 1
Piece of Life: Back to Hometown pt. 2
Piece of Life: Hillary, a Desperate Housewife
Lover's Smile pt. 1
Lover's Smile pt. 2
Lover's Smile pt. 3
Lover's Smile pt. 4
Dark Secrets
Dark Secrets II: A Long Sweet Night
Dark Secrets III: Too Fast to Die
Dark Secrets IV: Lost in the Echo
Dark Secrets V: One Step Closer
Dark Secrets VI: High Voltage

Revenge

Revenge II: Final Masquerade

Revenge: The Little Things You Give Me Away

Dark Lantern

Lily: The Story of a Call Girl, Part One

Lily: The Story of a Call Girl, Part Two

Lily: The Story of a Call Girl, Part Three

Lily Loves This Game

The Challenge for Lily

Lily Exceeds the Limit

The Bed Is Stained

Old Man & a Virgin

Jennifer's Nuptials

Dakota

Abused Billie: Part One

Abused Billie: Part Two

Rise of the Pervert

Jesslyn's Tragedy

Fall of the Pride

Home Alone

My Beloved Lecturer

Sex after Lunch

The Illicit Conspiracy

The Waiting Time

Quartet of Whiskers from the Abyss Within

Entangled Deceit: A Reflection on Second Chances

Echoes of Mortal Melodies in the New Realm of León

Echoes of Deceit: A Tapestry of Broken Hearts

About the Author

Frank Spreader is a passionate storyteller and martial arts enthusiast whose love for adventure and mystery has fueled a lifelong journey of writing. With a knack for blending intricate plots with dynamic characters, Frank crafts tales that captivate and inspire readers.

Growing up in a small town, Frank Spreader spent countless hours immersed in books and martial arts training, drawing inspiration from ancient legends and modern epics. This unique combination of interests shines through in his writing, where the disciplines of martial arts and the art of storytelling intersect to create vivid, action-packed narratives.

When not writing, Frank Spreader enjoys exploring nature, practicing martial arts, and delving into historical research. He believes in the power of perseverance and the importance of understanding one's roots, themes that often echo throughout his work.

Frank Spreader lives with his family in San Diego, where he continues to write and inspire others with tales of bravery, resilience, and the pursuit of justice. "The Vengeance of the Mighty" is his latest novel, a testament to the enduring spirit of those who fight for what they believe in.